jagged little pill

THE NOVEL

ERIC SMITH with **ALANIS MORISSETTE,**
DIABLO CODY, and **GLEN BALLARD**

Amulet Books
New York

Originally produced on Broadway by Vivek Tiwary, Arvind Ethan David, and Eva Price and Caiola Productions, Level Forward & Abigail Disney, Geffen Playhouse-Tenenbaum-Feinberg, James Nederlander, Dean Borell Moravis Silver, Stephen G. Johnson, Concord Theatricals, Bard Theatricals, M. Kilburg Reedy, 42nd.club, Betsy Dollinger, Sundowners, the Araca Group, Jana Bezdek, Len Blavatnik, BSL Enterprises, Burnt Umber Productions, Darren DeVerna & Jeremiah Harris, Daryl Roth, Susan Edelstein, FG Productions, Sue Gilad & Larry Rogowsky, Harmonia, John Gore Theatrical Group, Melissa M. Jones & Barbara H. Freitag, Stephanie Kramer, Lamplighter Projects, Christina Isaly Liceaga, David Mirvish, Spencer B. Ross, Bellanca Smigel Rutter, Iris Smith, Jason Taylor & Sydney Suiter, Rachel Weinstein, W.I.T. Productions/Gabriel Creative Partners, Independent Presenters Network, Universal Music Publishing Group, and Jujamcyn Theaters.

For Lyrics Credits, please see page 292.

Cataloging-in-Publication Data has been applied for and may be obtained from the Library of Congress.

ISBN 978-1-4197-5798-3

Printed and bound in U.S.A.
10 9 8 7 6 5 4 3 2 1

Amulet Books are available at special discounts when purchased in quantity for premiums and promotions as well as fundraising or educational use. Special editions can also be created to specification. For details, contact specialsales@abramsbooks.com or the address below.

ABRAMS The Art of Books
195 Broadway, New York, NY 10007
abramsbooks.com

For Erik Helewa.

You're the biggest fan
of this musical I know.

And I'm the biggest fan of you.

Chapter One

Frankie

I step out of my room and groan at the smell of pancakes. Between that and the sound of my mother's furious typing coming from the kitchen downstairs, I'm not sure what's going to be worse: her latest attempt at a Paleo breakfast or being subjected to the rough draft of a Christmas card she's been desperately trying to hone these last two weeks, sharpening her words and our family's accomplishments like a knife.

If you wield your loved ones like a blade, who are you fighting?

I squat down at the top of our stairs. I can hear her talking to herself over the keyboard, as well as my brother, Nick, clattering about in the bathroom behind me. She's definitely reading lines from the holiday letter again, muttering "Harvard" a little louder than everything else. There's a series of loud spritzing noises behind me, and just like that, the upstairs hallway reeks of a chocolate-scented body spray, despite the closed bathroom. My brother's "cologne" permeates even the thickest of wooden doors, and I am *not* riding with him to school today. That stuff will sink into my sweater and never leave.

I sigh and choose the lesser of two evil smells and make my way downstairs, my thick black combat boots loud against the hardwood steps.

"Frankie?" Mom ventures as I walk through the living room. The protest posters I was up late illustrating with Jo are still sprawled across our coffee table, a dozen bright neon markers popping against the earth tones of our home. Every piece of furniture is "reclaimed" or "repurposed" this or that, so Mom has a story to tell whenever one of her so-called friends from around the neighborhood or the school's PTA stops by.

Oh, this table? Rescued from a home that burned down. All proceeds went to the family, of course. The picture frames? So glad you noticed and asked. Built from the old gym floors of a shuttered YMCA. I sometimes imagine the stories the wood could tell, the people who walked on those boards, who played, who lived—

Ugh.

She looks up at me from behind her laptop in the kitchen, and I glance over at the countertop near the sink. It looks like a bakery exploded in here, several kinds of different flour bags sitting in various states of disarray, their contents spilled out over the cold gray marble.

Marble salvaged from a torn-down church, lest we all forget.

"Oh, good!" she exclaims, looking relieved. "Come here, come listen to this. I think I've finally got it."

She scoots her chair back, staring intently at the screen. She exhales, like this is some kind of performance, which, when it comes to Mom, almost everything is. I mean, it is *barely* seven in the morning, and she's already immaculately dressed, wearing a white button-down shirt and black slacks that somehow don't have flour all over them. Her blond hair is done up, her makeup is on point, and I wonder who she does all this for. It's certainly not for Dad, not with the way he grumbles around the house and falls asleep in the den. The two of them try to fake like everything is okay when I'm around, and I'm guessing whenever Nick is here, but for every forced softened expression there's a comment with a sharp barb, waiting to pierce the illusion.

I see right through them. And I've read enough novels and watched too many teen dramas to know that once Nick and I shuttle off to college, there's no way they are sticking together.

I just wish they'd rip the Band-Aid off now.

This wound isn't getting any better.

"Dear friends and family . . . Oh, wait! Do you want breakfast?" Mom asks, pointing at the middle of the kitchen table. There's a stack of pancakes that look a bit too thick, like someone tried to make flapjacks with the consistency of a Chicago deep-dish pizza. "I've got a plate for your brother over on the counter, but I know you like to choose your syrup."

"Yeah, sure," I say through a yawn, grabbing a plate and riffling through the cabinets for the syrup before checking the fridge. They're lined up in a rainbow: strawberry, marmalade, lemon, blueberry, a raspberry so purple it's almost black. But nothing green, because what would green syrup even be made of? Mint? Whatever concoction goes into a Shamrock Shake at McDonald's?

Sometimes . . . I wonder if Mom or Dad know. About me. About me and Jo, and how our night of crafting posters turned into an evening of snuggling and softly kissing on the couch when my family fell asleep. About how it's been more than just that one night, and more like a year of us tangled up in each other, secret moments and whispers when we can find them.

It's the little things like this, the syrup. Like Mom and Dad are signaling that they see me, that it's okay—or it's just another trend my mom spotted on Pinterest, I don't know. There's also the way she loves organizing the big bookshelf in the den according to color, a rectangular rainbow, big and bold, made up of the family's combined books. Dad's collection of Michael Crichton and Daniel H. Wilson, Nick's various Best American Essay collections I don't think he's ever read but that Mom keeps buying for him, my pile of books by Lamar Giles and Ashley Woodfolk, and Mom's massive collection of photo albums, thick as dictionaries.

Our family's story is the only one I really care about, she once said, when I asked her where *her* books were. I'd caught her running her hands over the spines of those photo albums, having just dusted the shelves, like the contents were something so terribly sacred.

She forgets I'm the adopted one.

And so much of my story is missing, simply not there for photographs. There's no pregnancy shoot with Mom and Dad, no newborn at the hospital pictures. I'm just suddenly there, the memory of my arrival wedged between a series of photos from Nick's third birthday and his first day of preschool. Like a commercial.

I haven't always felt so bitter about this. Being different in this house. Standing out. The Black girl in the white family. But lately, as these cracks keep forming, these fractures between Mom and Dad, the secrets I keep holding close to my chest—about Jo and about how I'm feeling, and how Nick just seems like he can't wait to get out of here—it's becoming almost easier to see things that way. I can't help but think how messed up that is, finding this comfort in knowing I don't belong here, in this family.

I grab the strawberry syrup and hope that a mix of this and endless powdered sugar will make the barely cooked dough Mom's trying to pass off as a pancake taste passable.

Pancakeable.

"Okay." Mom clears her throat. "Here we go."

I grab a seat and get to drowning my breakfast in sticky syrup.

"Dear friends and family, Merry Christmas from the Healy family!" Mom exclaims, like whoever is getting the letter is right here in the kitchen with us, or like she's on the phone. She reminds me a little of Jo when she's practicing one of her opening statements for Mr. Schneider and Mr. Hudacsko's speech and debate team at school, only instead of a carefully written speech about civil rights, it's a holiday card no one is going to read anyway. I've seen enough of her awful group of gossipy mom friends to know they pretend they care but don't really. They act more like they're in high school than Nick or I do. And we're *in* high school.

"We hope that you and yours are well," she continues. "Steve is loving his new role as partner at his firm, while Frankie—"

The syrup bottle lets out a loud *pbbbbttt*, spattering strawberry dribbles around my plate and on the table. I wince, and Mom sucks at her teeth before returning to her letter.

"*Frankie*," she stresses, and gives me a little smirk, "is busy with her art and social justice movements."

Her eyes flit over to me, looking for approval, and I shrug and nod, honestly a little surprised at the mention. She's not wrong, and she smiles and looks back at her computer as I take a bite of the pancakes . . . which do *not* get the same humoring endorsement. It's like accidentally getting a mouthful of sand after being knocked over by a wave at the beach, and just as salty. Why is there this much salt in these pancakes? I fake a yawn and spit the glob of not-quite-cooked batter into my hand and hide it in a napkin under my plate.

"And Nick, our sweet boy, just got the best news ever

this past week. He's been accepted into Harvard, early admission!" Mom sits back from the laptop, looking at the screen with pride, and wipes at what I guess are tears in the corners of her eyes. Jesus. That acceptance was a whole thing. This dreaded holiday letter could have been sent by now, but she wanted to wait to see if the news came in first, which only added to Nick's stress. He walks around the house like a boiling teakettle with a cork in it, eager and unable to scream.

"And as for me," she continues. "I'm still recovering a bit from the car accident in the summer, but I've got my loving family helping me get through—"

"There's my perfect wife."

Dad suddenly strolls in, interrupting, and leans down to give Mom a kiss . . . and she shifts away, her head shirking back sharply. I'm surprised to see him but not surprised at Mom's reaction. He completely deflates, mutters something I can't quite make out, and walks over to me, squeezing my shoulder. But even that gesture seems to have lost any of the joy he came into the room with. He's got a thin layer of stubble on his face and a red tint to his eyes, like he's had a hard night or just didn't sleep. Maybe both.

"Morning, kiddo," he says, yawning a little.

"Hey, Dad." I sigh, feeling bad for him.

"Steve, please, it's just . . . I haven't brushed my teeth yet," Mom says, adjusting herself in her seat, looking from me to him to her computer. "Do you want some coffee?"

"Sure." He sits down at the kitchen table with a huff as Mom gets up and fusses with the coffeemaker, the two of them moving up and down and away from each other in this devastating broken-family choreography. The Keurig pod hisses loudly, interrupting the awkward quiet.

The air in the room is just . . . so heavy.

I perk up when I hear Nick's feet thundering down the stairs, a short traditional pause followed by a boom, signifying him jumping down the last handful of steps. A routine as old as us, it feels. He's been leaping like that since we were kids, though lately, it feels like he's just been bounding further and further away from me. And it's not just him and his plans to move to Boston or Cambridge or wherever Harvard actually is. It's how much time he spends with his bros, in particular that rich douchebag, Andrew, and how he shows zero interest in Jo's and my events and protests, and how he just keeps drifting.

He's going to sail off in six months. Would it kill him to stay moored, stuck with me on this shore, just a little while longer?

"Dad?" Nick asks, walking toward the kitchen and lingering for a minute in the living room. He glances at me, confusion on his face, before looking back at Dad. "What are you doing here—"

"I can't be a little late for work to celebrate my son's college acceptance?" Dad beams. He gets up, brushing against Mom, who sucks at her teeth again.

"*What?*" he snaps, looking at her sharply. His tone sounds like a cracked whip.

"Nothing," Mom mutters. "Just . . . I almost spilled your coffee."

"Right."

Oh my God, I hate it here inside this powder keg. All this needless tension and passive aggression. And over what? It feels like it's all just gotten so much worse since Mom's accident. Little moments of quirky bickering about dishes or the lawn just got cranked up to eleven, with Dad just straight up not coming home from the office sometimes.

Dad turns back to Nick, a little smile peeking at the corner of his mouth. He unclasps the first few snaps on his wrinkly dress shirt, which looks slept in, and then tugs at it a little like Superman, revealing a HARVARD DAD shirt underneath. It's bright white with HARVARD in bold crimson lettering.

"Huh?" Dad grins, gesturing at the shirt. "What do you think?"

Nick glances at me, a knowing look of amusement on his face, and back at Dad. He laughs a little. "It's nice, Dad. It really is. I haven't even started yet. How did you get that shirt so fast?"

Nick finally strolls into the kitchen and grabs a chair next to me, shaking his head and nudging me with his arm. I nudge him back, and he pulls out his phone, tapping on the screen while looking at me. His whole getup is infuriating sometimes. The jeans, the Hollister shirts, the permanent bedhead that *somehow* he pulls off. He has this whole Nick Robinson look about him, the perfect mix of Mom and Dad, and being able to see that so clearly makes it even worse.

But as irritated as I am with him lately, I still love him.

"Oh please, I knew you were going to get in," Dad snorts. "I ordered it, like, two weeks ago."

"That's sweet, Steve," Mom says, but Dad just ignores her as she puts a mug in front of him.

It's so hard, watching this. It's bad enough I don't feel like I belong in this family, but the only family I really have is just crumbling apart. And instead of facing any of the tension or arguments head-on, they snap at each other and then act like nothing happened.

Nick nods at his phone, his eyes flashing a little as he looks at me.

I pull my phone out.

Nick: Is Jo upstairs?

I straight up push him this time, and he laughs a little. Asshole.

"No," I whisper to him with a bit of a snarl. I look up and Dad is reading something on his own phone, Mom back in front of her laptop. Nick nods, typing quickly, and my phone buzzes.

Nick: Just need to know if you need me to run interference. I got you.

He slides the phone back in his pocket, and a flash of warmth fills my chest. Even as he pushes away—with college, with his friends—every now and again he shows up for me. Little moments that say, *I'm still here.*

Mom's phone rings, that Wilson Phillips "one more day" song blasting. I wouldn't know this song if it wasn't for the fact that it's the ringtone set for all of Mom's friends. I swear, it's like their "live, laugh, love" anthem. I glance up at Dad, who is glaring at the phone, and when he catches me looking at him, he shrugs.

Mom answers the phone and puts it down on the table, on speaker.

"Hey, Libby!" Mom sings, as though we all aren't in the room. Dad grumbles something into his coffee.

"MJ!" Libby, better known as Mrs. Porter, exclaims. "Just checking in to make sure you've got everything you need for the fundraiser."

"I think I can handle a few dozen cupcakes, Libs." Mom laughs, looking over at me and Nick as though we're somehow in on the joke.

"Okay, just remember we need them on time. And nothing store-bought, the kids and parents can tell."

"Ugh," Mom groans. "The cupcakes from the spring were not store-bought, how many times do I have to—"

"All right, love, I have to get going!" Mrs. Porter interrupts, and Mom leans back in her chair. "See you at the meeting!"

"Okay, I'll—"

And the line goes dead.

"She's always so busy!" Mom looks over at Dad, rolling her eyes. "Can you imagine?"

"I cannot," Dad snorts, putting his phone down, his demeanor shifting noticeably, like he's getting ready to give me or Nick a talking-to about a failing grade. But instead of looking at either of us, he turns his attention back to Mom. "MJ, you know . . . you really deserve friends who aren't too busy to have a conversation."

"Oh, shush." Mom waves him off, focusing back on her laptop. "We talk."

"Do you?" he asks. "Or does she just talk *at* you?"

Mom exhales through her nose and zeroes back in on the screen. That chat is apparently over. But Dad's right—I've noticed it, and even Nick has brought it up once or twice, whenever one of them stops by. How Mom's friends don't really feel like friends but like . . . I don't know, a clique of popular girls who never got over ruling the hallways of their school, so now they try to rule over a suburb.

"Well!" Nick exclaims, slapping his hands on the table, breaking all the awkwardness in the air. What am I supposed to do when he's not here to do that? "I'm hungry, so . . ."

He leans over the table, looking at the stack of pancakes in the center. He glances at me, and I shake my head. The least I can do is try to warn him. He reaches out anyway, plopping a few of the pancakes—sandcakes, really—onto his plate.

His funeral.

"Oh, wait! Just a second . . ." Mom says, getting back up from her laptop. She hurries over to the counter and quickly returns, a plate in her hand. She places it gently in front of Nick, beaming brightly.

I squint at the pancakes. They don't look any better than the ones on the kitchen table, and there's something written on them in what looks like blueberry syrup.

"Why does it say 'Dick' on them?" I ask.

Nick sputters out a laugh.

"Frankie, come on," Dad protests, still looking down at his phone. Even when they're at each other's throats, Dad still comes to her defense over little things. Like making fun of her syrup penmanship.

"What?! No, it doesn't!" Mom gasps, leaning over the table. "'Nick.' That's an 'N.' Just . . . not a great 'N.'" She storms back over to her chair, but before she sits down, she sets her eyes on me. Her eyebrows furrow down, and she glances around the table, tsk-tsking.

Great.

Here we go.

I can see it happening, another one of her mood shifts. Another side effect of her recovery post-accident? Her frustrations with her not-quite-friends? Or just extra rage pouring over from whatever she and Dad have been going through these last few months? I don't know. All I know is she's a warm and bubbly Instagram mom one minute, then a cold and easily set off will-probably-end-up-going-viral-for-yelling-in-the-supermarket mom the next.

And I know it. I *know* she's like this now. But why should I have to change who I am to avoid whatever this wrath is she's hurling at me and Dad, while never sending any of those vibes at Nick? It's not fair that I'm the only one caught in the crossfire of her and Dad's fights.

"It's *December*, Frankie."

"I'm aware of the month?" I'm not sure where she's going with this one.

"Apparently your shorts aren't," she snips.

Ah. There it is.

"Oh, come on," I groan. "It's hot in school. They blast the heat like we're all going to freeze." I glance over at Nick, hoping for some acknowledgment, but he just pokes at his pancakes.

"I'm sure you can find some jeans upstairs?"

"MJ," Dad says, looking up at Mom from his phone for a flash, an exhausted expression on his face.

"What?!" Mom snaps.

"Do we have to get into all this?!" he groans, leaning back in his chair. It squeaks against the tiled floor, and Mom winces, like she feels the pain of the ceramic. "I didn't call out of work this morning to listen to you fight with the kids over nothing and have you bickering at me."

"Well, I'm sorry, but how you present yourself to the world matters," Mom retorts, glaring at him. "Especially when you're a young woman."

"Nick," I whisper, elbowing him, wanting him to tag in and just say something. Anything. "You know how hot it gets inside the cafeteria—"

"Anyone want more syrup?" Nick asks, shifting a little in his seat, like he's thinking about getting up.

So much for him showing up for me. I reel back at Mom, glaring at her.

"You're so focused on my shorts but haven't even asked

about my signs in the living room. *That* is something that matters, and it's more important than just that small aside in your stupid Christmas card. Not what I'm wearing."

I jump out of my seat, and Nick sighs, resigning himself back into his chair. I stomp my way into the living room and pluck one of the poster board signs off the couch, which flaps about, making a funny noise in the hustle.

"SMAAC is protesting in the cafeteria today." I hold the sign out.

Mom exhales.

"*Does my period blood scare you?*" she asks but also reads, her tone as flat as the paper the sign is made of. It's just one of several Jo and I spent all night working on. "What are you even protesting? Is someone anti-periods? What's SMAAC?"

"Social Movements and Advocacy Committee," Nick says before I do. I can't help but look at him, surprised. I didn't realize he knew what it actually stood for. "Frankie started it with Jo this year."

"Are you in it too?" Mom asks, sounding slightly aghast.

"Well, no, not really—" Nick starts.

"And what if he was?" I ask, glaring at her. "Would that be so wrong?"

I mean, he's definitely not in the club. I've asked him, and he's come to two meetings, but I think that was mostly to talk to girls there. And that interest quickly faded when the only people in the club at the second meeting were me and Jo. I'd join the other social movement club at school, but I've never really gotten along with those girls. Back in junior high, me and another adopted kid, this Indian girl named Rebecca, "didn't really count" to them as people of color, having white parents and all. I got in a fight with one of them and was suspended for a week.

Whatever. I'd do it again.

We're all older now, wiser and all that. But you don't forget those kinds of moments, and I don't need them to be my friends. Rebecca ended up at a private Catholic school. I wonder if it's any better there for her.

"There's nothing wrong with standing up for your beliefs, Frankie," Mom says, sounding worn out. She rubs her hand over her face. "Look, when I was in high school, me and my friends were just like you and Jo."

A little snorting laugh escapes Nick, and despite how terribly unhelpful he's being, I can't help the smirk that cracks my face.

"I . . . seriously doubt that." I glance over at Nick, and he looks away, his face twisted up in a pained trying-not-to-laugh expression.

"Well, we were!" Mom exclaims, gesturing at my sign. Nick snorts again. "We made signs, we hosted bake sales, we had sit-ins. There were these woods in back of our old school that were home to saltmarsh sparrows, which are critically endangered in Connecticut, I'll have you know. So, we were fighting to stop them from developing back there."

"Really?" I ask, feeling a little impressed. "That's . . . actually awesome. What happened? Where was that?"

"Well—" Mom starts.

"They cleared the woods," Dad chimes in, still looking at his phone.

"Goddamn it, Steve," Mom snaps. "That doesn't matter. What matters is we were fighting for something, even if we didn't really win. We got attention. And that still counts as making a difference."

"Birds are dead," Dad says matter-of-factly.

"Steve!" Mom shouts, and Nick sputters out a laugh again before clearing his throat and swiping at the tears pricking his eyes. Dad smirks. "You're not helping, Nick. And I'm not sure that all of this—how you're dressing, these . . . *confrontational* signs—is giving off the image you want it to, Frankie."

"Image?! Confrontational? Well, this is what I'm doing." I hand her my sign and she drops it on the table. "Just because it's about having free tampons in the bathrooms and not about some fucking birds doesn't make it any less important."

"Frankie, watch your language," Dad says.

"You're the one instigating! And come to think of it, where were you when Jo and I were in the civil rights protests last year? You can show up for birds but not racism?"

"Oh, come on, Frankie." Mom sighs, sounding exhausted. "You know we're anti-racists in this house. We don't see color."

"Mom!" Nick exclaims.

"Jesus, MJ." Dad buries his face in his hands.

"What?" Mom asks, perplexed. "We don't!"

"We'll unpack that later." I glare at Mom, and she shakes her head, looking away. Mercifully, the tension in the room is interrupted by my phone's alarm. It's time to head off to school, and if I want to get there without requiring a ride from my brother, who smells like a college dorm room party, I'll have to get going.

I take my sign and walk back into the living room, gathering the rest of the poster boards.

"Frankie," Mom presses.

I grab my tote bag off the coffee table and start shoveling the markers inside—supplies that Jo left behind. They rattle against the books inside, a beat-up paperback of *Great Expectations* taking the brunt of the attack. Oh, Estella. I feel you sometimes. Raised in a place where you feel you don't belong that also makes sure you know it, so you lash out.

"Frankie, wait, did you want a ride?" Nick asks.

"*Now* you want to help?" I snap back, pushing open the front door.

"We're not done talking about this!" Mom shouts, as I hitch my bag up.

"Swing by the protest later," I say, turning around to glare at Nick. "I'll save you a sign."

And with that, I'm out the door.

Jo: Hey, I haven't seen you all morning. Where are you?

Jo: I miss you, jerk. ♥

Frankie: Sorry, MJ was having another one of her meltdowns.

Frankie: I can't wait to get the hell out of there.

Jo: I know how you feel.

Frankie: ♥

Jo: Are we still meeting up before lunch?

Jo: Wasn't sure if you brought the signs or not.

Jo: Maybe we could work on a few more if no one shows up at the meeting . . .

Jo: Or pretend to. 😉

Frankie: Oh my God, Jo.

Jo: You love it.

Frankie: I have them! I'll meet you before free period in the usual spot.

Jo: Have you heard about this party?

Frankie: Did you forget who you are talking to?

Jo: Right, right. My mistake. Andrew Montefiore is having a bash at his house tomorrow night.

Frankie: That sounds terrible.

Jo: Could be fun. Free drinks. Kelsey and her crew are going to be there, and I think they'd really be into SMAAC if we just spent some time with them.

Frankie: Just into SMAAC? Is that all?

Jo: Oh, shut up. It's just you and me, remember?

Frankie: Me and you.

Jo: You and me.

Chapter Two

The fun thing about the hallway once school is out, or hell, even when it's in session in between classes, is the people-watching. You can figure out pretty quickly who is using who, who is fooling around behind someone's back, when and where the next big house party is going to be. And right now, leaning against the cold brick wall outside Mr. Martinho's classroom, I'm observing the masses while waiting for Frankie.

The early Christmas gift I got for her is digging into my leg, and I'm eager to give it to her. That and wrap her up in my arms when we're finally alone in the classroom. I almost hope we get no new members today.

I give the door a little nudge. It's open and unlocked. Our club isn't exactly approved by the school board, because of membership rules (two official people a club does not make) and our often "volatile" subject matter (protests that embarrass the less-than-liberal teachers and parents here). But it's nice to have a young history teacher who makes space for us. Oh, Mr. Martinho, you rebel. My parents would hate you, and that only makes you cooler.

It's free period, a brief moment of respite before lunch, when most of the student body hangs out in homerooms, the library, or the cafeteria. Supposedly some kids hit the gym for sports and, like, working out. I've never seen it and never will—free weights and treadmills are not for me—but I believe it.

I spot Swapna and Preeti walking with bags from Wendy's gripped in their hands, which tells me they either cut their last class to make the mad dash to the downtown area a quarter mile from our school, or maybe missed the entire first half of the day. With winter break almost here, it's not surprising. Teachers always seem to start caring less and less about cutting class and other nonsense that doesn't actually matter as vacation looms.

I can't quite see Andrew, David, or Lily, but I can hear them making their way down the hallway beyond the students currently milling about. I've been around them enough, particularly at Frankie's when they're hanging with Nick, to recognize that trio's voices together. They're like a really shitty pop band trying to harmonize, their gossip and boasting playing off one another, but all I hear is feedback.

And then there's Nick and Bella.

It's hard not to see how smitten Nick is with her. The confidence that he seems to radiate around school and even at the Healys' house—all that cockiness while driving his car or holding court with his bros outside—it just evaporates. And right here, standing next to her across the way, he even looks a little shorter. It's probably just from the way he's angled, I'm aware, but part of me thinks that bravado makes him a few inches taller, and Bella just makes it crumble away.

It's sweet, sort of.

He's in his usual dark jeans that look like they've had one too many days on the beach, even though we're nowhere near one, and he keeps running his hand through his permanently windswept hair. And Bella, she's got this soft, kissable smile that betrays her whole punk rock, leather-jacket-wearing aesthetic. She pulls the jacket closer to her as Nick leans against the wall, like he might be able to disappear into the concrete if he pushes hard enough. They're close to something, those two. You can see it, and I wonder if anything is ever going to happen with them before they jet-set off to college in six months. Not that I terribly care, but he is my best friend's brother. Hard not to feel a little invested in whatever his drama is.

I fuss with the little gift I got for Frankie, tucked away in my pocket. I hope she likes it. With how serious my family takes Christmas, it's not likely I'll get to see her on the holiday, even if we do live a quick bike ride away from each other.

The bell rings, the same weird buzzing drone we've been listening to these past few years, and Nick straightens up and glances over at me. He gives me a little nod and walks over, Bella trailing him.

"You hear about this one?" Bella asks, bumping against Nick. "Harvard?"

"Yeah," I snort. "It's Frankie's hot topic of the week."

"Is she . . ." Nick looks around and back at me, his brow furrowed. "Is she okay? She kinda bolted this morning and hasn't really answered any of my texts. I think she's mad at me."

"Ask her yourself." I nod behind them. Frankie is walking our way, posters in hand, a fraying tote bag over her arm. There's a pile of books illustrated on the side, the name "A Novel Idea" screened on it—a bookstore we visited on our class trip to Philadelphia freshman year. The bag has seen better days, much like Frankie and her family.

"Hey, where have you been?" Nick asks, as Frankie hustles by him, ducking into Mr. Martinho's classroom. She peeks back out and looks at me.

"Did you hear something?" Frankie asks, looking around the hall as if no one is there. "Weird."

"Oh, come on!" Nick exclaims, and then looks at me and over at Bella. "What am I supposed to do here?"

"Just . . . give her a minute to cool down. You know how she is," I say, looking into the class. Frankie's laying the posters out over the teacher's desk and emptying her tote full of markers and notepads.

"Fine," Nick grumbles. "You coming to Andrew's party tomorrow night?"

"What?" I laugh. "Me? No. Maybe. I don't know."

"It'll be fun," Bella presses, giving me a playful nudge. We don't know each other terribly well, but I like her. She's one of those people I wish I'd taken the time to get to know better, but now with her and Nick's graduation looming, I feel like maybe it's a bit too late. Maybe we can reconnect on social media or something, like so many people seem to do in every Netflix teen drama I've seen.

"That's debatable." I roll my eyes. Though in reality, I kinda want to go. I do. I heard Kelsey is going, this girl I'm convinced would be a great addition to our club and also just exudes this wild coolness that I'm eager to learn from, with her half-buzzed bright reddish-orange hair and lip ring. We went to summer camp together ages ago, and she's since grown into one of the coolest girls here, while I'm just . . . well, me. And besides, nothing wrong with a few more friends.

"Well, be sure to tell her about it," Nick says. "I'll, um, catch you later, J."

"You don't want to stay?" I ask, but he and Bella are already walking away. He looks over his shoulder, giving me a look that says I should know better. And I should. The hallway is mostly cleared out at this point, though I spot a few students toward the other end, making their way out of the building. Probably seniors, wrapping up with early schedules. A door to a classroom next door creaks open, and Mrs. Podos, one of the dance teachers, steps out, exhaling loudly. She catches me looking and ducks back into her classroom.

I get it, though.

Everyone is stressed out about something. Someone. As the year wraps up and the holidays approach, it can feel like you're running out of time to make things happen, even though the new year offers up exactly that. A new year. A time to shake things up. Hm. Maybe it isn't too late to connect with Bella. I wonder if it's too late for me, and all these questions I have about myself. Will it be easier after high school, or should I go full New Year, New Me come January?

The door opens again, and I half expect to see Mrs. Podos hustling out with a carton of cigarettes, making for the parking lot where students and teachers who smoke all meet on common ground, but instead it's Kelsey Nicolau. She's slinging her backpack over her shoulder, dancing gear in a little duffel bag on her hip. She practically floats down the hallway, like a punk rock ballerina stepping out of a music video for A Day to Remember.

"Kelsey!" I shout. My voice cracks a little, and I feel my cheeks flush with embarrassment. *Get it together, Jo.* She turns and looks at me, a little smile quirking on her face. "Do you, uh, have a minute? We're having the . . . you know, the club . . ."

Oh God, what is happening to me? I feel like I'm sweating. If she does stay, that takes care of any alone time I'm hoping to steal with Frankie, but . . . I can't help myself.

"Ah," Kelsey says with a little rueful look on her face. "Can't this time, Fabrics, but maybe next week? Some of the dancers are getting coffee."

"Yeah, totally." I nod. She is the only person on the entire planet who can call me "Fabrics"—a bad reference to my full name, "Joanne," and that craft store—and get away with it. I think if anyone in my family tried it, or even Frankie, I'd probably lose it. But for some reason, that little nickname coming out of her mouth just *sends* me.

"You could come if you want?" She gestures down the hallway, like the coffee shop is right there. "I wouldn't mind the extra company."

Her eyebrow quirks up, and it feels like the hallway is getting narrower.

"Oh, no, I can't, I have . . ." I glance back at the classroom, at Frankie getting ready. "The club meeting and all."

"It's all right, next time." And just like that, she's off down the hallway in a twirl. A little wave of guilt crests over me. My girlfriend is right behind me, and here I am, falling apart over my eternal unrequited crush, whom I've been swooning over since junior high.

It's just a silly, flustery crush, though. That's allowed. Not like I'm doing anything about it, or ever would if I could. Kelsey is out of reach, like a Christmas decoration on top of a tree. Beautiful to look at, but I'm not capable of making that stretch. Honestly, I'm not even sure how someone like Frankie Healy has fallen for me. She is exquisite, and even though I tell her this all the time, and hear much the same back, I still don't feel like I'm quite enough.

How does anyone grow into believing they deserve anything? When does that happen?

I walk into the classroom, and Frankie is busy sorting out the posters. She's gritting her teeth, like she's working out and not just moving paper around.

"So . . . rough day?" I ask, trailing the edge of the desk with my finger.

Her eyes flit up and she exhales, shaking her head.

"I'm taking that as a yes?"

"It's just more of MJ," she huffs, and sits on the desk, patting the surface. I sit next to her, and she leans in, kissing me softly, giving my lower lip a small nibble. She sighs. That was the exact moment I was hoping to pluck away from the time we've got in here.

"This. This is where I want to live. Not in that house." She reaches out and runs her thumb over my lips and down to my chin. "Right there."

"Yeah." I exhale, the guilt of eyeing up Kelsey irking its way through my chest. "Maybe one day. Did something happen with Nick?" I nod at the door to the classroom, like he's still there.

"No," she groans. "Yes? I don't know. He's fine, but MJ had this meltdown at home, and he didn't really have my back, and . . ." She shakes her head. "I guess that's not totally true. He was worried you might have been still upstairs and wanted to plot out a way to get you out without MJ or Dad seeing."

"Really?!" I sputter out a laugh.

"Yeah." She smiles a little and then her brow furrows. "But he's still leaving. And he's still spending all that time away with his friends, and every day MJ finds a new way to remind me that Nick is her greatest accomplishment and I'm the adoption fail—"

"Frankie, come on." I sigh. "You know he's going through his own shit right now too. With your mom, and honestly, probably with you."

"Shut up." Frankie playfully scowls at me, squinting her eyes. She softens. "You're right. I know you're right."

"It'll be okay. I'll still be here, you know?"

"Me and you?"

"You and me."

I look out toward the empty classroom, all the barren seats, the walls with pops of color from all of Mr. Martinho's posters. References to historical young adult books he keeps trying to get us all to read and people from history he thinks we should be familiar with. Thankfully, not a collection of dead white guys, but poets from the Harlem Renaissance and modern icons of queer resistance. Couldn't ask for a better history teacher, truly.

It's our club enrollment that could use some improvement.

"So . . . full house?" I nod at the chairs, and Frankie bumps her shoulder into me.

"People will show up for this thing eventually."

"It's December." I laugh. "The year is half over."

"Listen, we're an indie sleeper hit, thank you very much. SMAAC is only available on vinyl." Frankie grins and her smile deflates a little. "Sorry I . . . earlier. I know I shouldn't complain about my parents, but—"

"Shh." I shake my head. "Your feelings there are valid, even if most of your mom's drama has to do with her melting down over getting the wrong salad delivered from Grubhub."

"I just can't believe she got worked up about these." Frankie tugs a little at her shorts, which look great, halfway hidden by her thick, multicolored knit sweater, fraying at the bottom edges. There's a little enamel Haim pin on one of the pockets that makes me smile, from a concert we snuck off to last year at Mathur College's freshman orientation festival, just a ten-minute drive away from us. It was the first time I felt like we were really shifting away from being best friends to something a little bit more, as she held my hand while they performed "Now I'm in It."

A song about not being able to pretend you're just friends anymore. God. It was so on the nose that it hurt.

"Like, yes, it's December, but it's also almost seventy degrees outside," she continues. "Might as well enjoy the climate crisis."

"You *do* have on a sweater." I grin.

"Shut up." She laughs, swatting at me again.

"It could be worse, you know. Your mom just yells at you. Mine prays. 'Dear Jesus, please guide my daughter through her temporary teenage identity crisis. And may she emerge as the straight Disney princess femme-bot I always dreamed she would be. In the name of Fox News, amen.'" I glance back up at Frankie, a little smile cracking at the corner of her mouth.

"She's still holding out hope, huh?"

"This morning she was like, 'Why would you choose to look like that?' And I'm like, 'Why would you choose to look like the Talbots catalog threw up on you?'"

Frankie sputters out a laugh, which cracks a smile out of me. It's hard, though, all this. I just want to be . . . myself, whoever that is. My mom doesn't see me entirely, and really, Frankie doesn't either. But I'm not sure I'm ready to *be* completely seen.

"I want you to talk about your frustrations, I do . . . but there's a difference between thinking your shorts are too short and thinking your clothes are 'too gay,' as my mom says."

"Jo—"

I wave her off, hopping off the desk. It's my mom's usual snarky remark to my enamel-pinned-up jean jackets and track pants, thrift store T-shirts and beanies.

"It's fine." I always say that. *It's fine.* And it is. At least for the two of us. It's not fine for me, but I don't want Frankie, my best friend and . . . girlfriend, I think? I don't know, we've yet to say it out loud, but I know how I've come to define us these last few months. The last thing I want is her feeling like she can't talk about her problems at home, even if she thinks they pale in comparison with mine. Because while her mom might make everything into some kind of contest with winners and losers, that's not what this is.

It's just different.

And that's okay.

I put one hand in my pocket and pull out the gift I've been waiting to give her today. An early Christmas present. I know my parents, and we'll be taking the long drive to visit my various uncles and aunts in New Jersey and staying out there for who knows how many days. Not much to look forward to there, save for unwrapping whatever not-great-but-well-intentioned presents the people in my family have half forgotten to get me. Last year someone got me a bowie hunting knife. The year before, a handle of Grey Goose vodka, like I wasn't underage. The brass of Frankie's gift is cold in my hand and between my fingers, and I hold the fountain pen up and out to her like a magic wand.

"Surprise." I smile.

"What's this?" she asks, reaching out to take it like it's something precious. Before I can answer she uncaps it and gasps, turning to me, her eyes wide. "Jo!"

"For your journals and poems and stuff." I shrug and fish out a small box the size of a tiny matchbox. "There are some ink wells in here too, for when it goes dry. Which it will quickly, knowing you." A bit of warmth fills my cheeks under her gaze, after she takes the box and looks up at me. It's unfair, the way she looks at me like that.

Like I'm everything, in these little stolen moments. In an empty history classroom with a club that has no membership. Late at night, on her parents' couch, a living room lit by streetlamps outside and iPhones on a coffee table. Hands brushing between classes in a hallway.

I wonder when we can stop stealing them.

Chapter Three

Phoenix

As far as lies go, I think the whole "you'll make friends fast!" line is one of the biggest Mom has ever handed out, paired right up there with how my hamster, Antonio, went to go "live on a farm" in third grade. I get the intention behind it, the love that's there and meant to reassure me. But it doesn't make the truth hurt less once it inevitably bubbles to the surface.

Like how when you're the "new kid" people don't exactly throw themselves at you, pleading for your friendship. No one has come barreling down the hall, begging to be my new best friend, save for this kid Nick who wants me to come to some party tomorrow night. No, those people are back home in Danbury. Patrick, Saundra, Lisa, Nwayieze, Mitchell . . . all ever-present in my texts and social media feeds, while we're here for the next, well, however long it takes for Ruby to get better.

If she gets better.

I shake the thought away and try to get comfortable

in my seat at the back of this classroom. The walls are like a monument to the students here and those who have come before, fading pages full of typewritten text tucked away behind glass display cases, next to crisp white papers with oddly formatted sentences. Poetry, probably, though I can't really read any of it from here. The entire classroom smells like ink and old paper, and I wonder how the teacher has managed that. It's just printer paper behind that glass, and there isn't exactly a collection of vintage books on the shelves here. Whatever the mystery of the smell is, it's a pretty significant contrast from the rest of the school, which mostly has this just-cleaned Lysol scent nearly everywhere. Even the gym.

Back at home, our gym at least had the decency to smell like old socks and soon-to-be-crushed dreams. And back there, students were always on time for class.

How am I the only one here?

And who shows up early for a creative writing class where they have absolutely nothing to present? I pull out my phone and flip through my feeds and end up scrolling through Saundra's Bookstagram, shot after artfully taken shot of what she's been reading lately, arranged with flowers and candles and fanciful paper. Something called washi tape that she spends a lot of her money on. With the amount of care she puts into those pictures of books, I just know she's going to do the same when she starts writing them.

God, I miss our little writing group. Our favorite coffee shop downtown, Locke and Tea, with all the little padlocks on the fencing outside. Our poems that were clear overshares, read with earnestness over way-too-sugary lattes and tea doused full of honey. The owners and their cats that seemed more like dragons, with different-colored eyes, and that moved like liquid smoke between tables and chairs and legs.

I rummage through my backpack, plucking out a beat-up notebook I've carried with me just about everywhere since I started school. I flip it open toward the back, my scrawled-out poems and attempts at short stories staring at me from the weathered pages. This notebook has seen some things, but then again, so have I.

I run my hand over a note in the margins, on the latest poem I'd been working on.

This is good. Keep going.

The handwriting, all awkward and a little all over the place, is Ruby's. From just a few days ago, when we got her situated in the hospital. She's always asking to read whatever I'm kicking around, and her bright red pen shines out against the black-inked pages in the best way possible. It's not a grade or a mark.

It's an exclamation.

It also reminds me that I need to scan in the last bundle of pages. I do my best to make sure I do that as often as possible. Mom makes us watch this old Christmas movie, *Love Actually*, every December, and it has successfully scarred me for life. There's this scene where Colin Firth has his whole hand-typed novel blown into the air and into a lake, and he had no copies.

No copies? What kind of psychopath does that?

I pick up my phone to take a photo with my scanning app, when the bell rings, a weird low droning sound that startles me in my seat. It's going to take me a really long time to get used to that here. Back at home, the bell was this merry-sounding thing, and here it sounds like a funeral dirge.

Suddenly the hallway outside the classroom is bursting with life. Some students filter into the room, talking to one another in quick, flitting bursts, wrapping up conversations, taking seats. Every single person is a new face and vanishes just as quickly from my memory as folks who walk by me on the street do. I sit and stare at the back of two dozen heads, some of them already bowing down and fussing over some writing. It's just a lot of hair and shoulders hidden by jackets and sweaters, as the teacher fumbles her way in through the door, a massive bundle of papers and books in her arms. She flops everything onto the metal desk with a loud bang, jostling the would-be writers out of their focus.

"Whew," she says, huffing and sitting on her desk. "Sorry I'm a little bit late, my darlings. Had to make copies of your pieces and there was a line at the printer. Miss Vicente was photocopying *algebra* assignments."

A number of students boo at the mention of algebra, and the writing teacher grins. That's the name of the teacher whose class I had earlier today, where I met that

Nick kid. I look around the room for his . . . I don't know. Jacket? Backpack? I don't see anyone who looks like him, though.

The teacher digs in her desk and pulls out two enormous candles and sets them on the surface. She walks over to the classroom door and peers outside, before shutting it and lowering a little shade over the classroom door window. That's when she pulls out a lighter and lights those candles, and after a second or two, the room smells powerfully of old paper again.

I squint at the big candles and make out "used bookstore" as the smell.

Hm. Neat. Though I suspect the cautious stepping around the door and shade probably have to do with open flames being a big no-no in schools. Back at my old high school, this guy Andres in one of my history courses tried to make his girlfriend, Darlene, swoon on Valentine's Day with candles and flowers in an empty classroom and set off all the smoke alarms. We had to have a whole assembly about it. Andres. What a legend. Always doing over-the-top romantic things that ended somewhat poorly. I wonder what he's up to now.

The teacher wafts a little of the smoke from the candles with her hand and glances up at the room, squinting a little, before she settles on me. Her eyes go wide.

"Ah!" she exclaims, walking my way.

Oh, great. I hurry and shut my notebook, shoving it back into my pack.

"Seems like we have a new student." She stops at my

desk, and the entire class turns in their seats to stare at me. Their uniform shuffling sounds like a battalion of soldiers shifting formation in a war movie. I press myself back into my chair, like maybe if I push hard enough I can vanish into the wood and steel, but most of them turn back around just as fast, interest lost.

"Miss Rishi," she says, placing a pen and a notebook on my desk. I'm confused, and she must catch my expression. "Every student gets a Moleskine notebook at the start of the class, to fill up as our time together wears on. I'm sorry you're here for the last week of our class, but it didn't feel right not to give you one."

I reach out and take the notebook, the surface of the cover rough and a little scratchy. Is this teacher rich or something? These kinds of notebooks are expensive, and how many classes does she have? Black and simple, paired with a gel pen, these books are still, like, what, twenty bucks a pop? It's hard not to be immediately struck by the gift that, really, this teacher gives to everyone, when it's the last thing either of my parents would give to me. Dad always thought the writing group was impractical. *Take up a hobby that could become a proper job.* Writing wasn't that. Mom's at least a bit more encouraging, but that's because she sees me every day. Dad, more or less on holidays. Definitely on the less side of things.

With Ruby's medical bills piling up and this move to a new city for better, longer-stay treatment, everything my mom and dad do revolves around planning for the most cost-effective way to keep us afloat. And this notebook just reminds me that I really need to take a stroll downtown to start hunting for any kind of retail job, to help support Mom in our new home. Dad's never late with support, I'll give him that much. Nothing about our situation is like a Lifetime movie or anything. But he didn't come with us, and Mom is solo in a new town, while he's off on the West Coast someplace, and Ruby is in the hospital.

Hm. Maybe it is a little Lifetime-movie-ish. Though his girlfriend would have to turn out to be a murderer or something.

You're gonna have to contribute, Dad said, before we moved. Like he was coming along and would be pitching in to do the actual work, but that's not the case at all. He's far away, not dealing with what's happening to Ruby and what's going on with our little family as a result of his absence. We're all just falling apart.

Sigh. I'm trying.

"Thanks," I say to Miss Rishi, forcing myself to sound grateful regardless of all these swirling feelings. When I open the notebook, it makes that satisfying crunch noise that new journals often do.

"There's a lot of time between now and then," Miss Rishi says, tapping a blank page of the journal with a well-manicured hot-pink nail. "Whether we're talking about the year ending or this time you have in high school."

I glance up at her.

"You live, you learn. Fill it up." She smiles.

I smile back just as the classroom door flies back open, hitting the wall with a bang. A girl wearing a fraying multicolored sweater, shorts, and large combat boots walks in, a few books in hand, and looks at the door with a wince. "Excuse me."

She shrugs, then weaves her way through the chairs and desks. I glance around and realize the only free seat left is right next to me, and it sends my lonely heart racing. She is . . . dauntingly beautiful. And for a moment, just a moment, her eyes flit up toward mine, and I look away so fast I feel my neck crack. I take a quick glimpse at her as she settles into her seat, placing some of her books on the desk.

There's a weathered copy of *Great Expectations* and books of poetry by Maggie Smith and Janet McNally, which both look equally beaten up in the way loved books often are. There's the sound of someone clearing their throat, and I glance up from the books to see her staring at me.

"Sorry," I mumble, looking away.

"Frankie," she says, and I turn back. She nods at me a little. "You new?"

"Yeah," I say, and she snorts out a little laugh. "What?"

"Welcome to Thunderdome." She shakes her head. "You sharing anything from in there?"

"Oh." I tap the Moleskine, thinking of the poem I was fussing over during lunch, tucked away in my notebook from home. "No, Miss Rishi just gave it to me. She seems nice."

"Yeah, everyone here loves her." Frankie nods and then smirks. "Can't speak for the rest of the class being nice, though. Buckle up."

She gets out her own notebook, which is stickered in a wide array of symbols and slogans that I can't quite make out, looking like a graffitied wall that's been painted over again and again. She pulls out a gorgeous brass fountain pen and gives it a little shake, and I feel my eyes go wide. Saundra had a similar one back at home.

She starts to write with it and jerks her hand back, sucking at her teeth.

"Ugh!" She holds a hand up, ink splashed on her palm. She smears it and it leaves a streak of dark blue.

"You, um"—I lean over—"have to avoid touching the feed?"

"What?" she asks, looking over at me, brow furrowed.

"It's the . . ." I awkwardly point, and she holds out her pen. I take it, and it has a lot of weight to it. "Wow. This is nice. But here." I turn the pen toward her, pointing at the nib at the end. "See under here? This is the feed for the fountain pen, where the ink flows and a bit gets stored. But it's a sensitive area. If you press too hard, it can stain you."

"Huh," Frankie says, reaching out and taking the pen again. Our fingers brush in the exchange, and my heart flutters again. She points the pen at me. "Thanks."

"No problem." I smile and look down at my hand.

It's stained with ink.

I rub the leftover ink between my fingers. Oh, I really want to get to know this girl.

"All right, let's get started," Miss Rishi says, sitting on her desk at the front of the classroom, snapping me back

41

into the here and now. Everything about her screams "cool writing teacher," from her jeans that have enamel pins along the pockets to what looks like a band T-shirt. She adjusts her thick glasses and shuffles some of the papers in her hands, grinning at the classroom.

"So . . . any volunteers?" Her smile goes wide and she pulls a single sheet out, her eyes scanning it. "Today, we've got Jeff, Megan, Frankie, and Stephanie for peer review. But before we start all that, we've got a new voice joining us. I'd like to welcome Phoenix Vargas. Stand up, Mr. Vargas. Tell the class a little about yourself."

Everyone shifts in their seats again, and my heart catches in my chest.

I look over at Frankie, a smile on her perfect face.

"Uh . . . sure." I swallow and stand up. "I'm, uh, Phoenix. I moved here from Danbury about a week ago, we've been getting settled in, I guess. I like writing a lot, which is why I signed up to be in here for my only week of the year. I read and skateboard, but not at the same time."

Frankie snorts out a laugh. No one else does.

Tough crowd.

"And yeah, I just spend a lot of time with my mom and sister when I can. I'm a little boring, I guess."

"I doubt that," Miss Rishi says, smiling. "And what do you like to write?"

"Poems, mostly. Some short stories." I curl my toes up in my sneakers, starting to feel a bit anxious. "Sorry, I don't have anything to share, really."

"Maybe you'll find something." She glances back at

her paper and then up at me. "Thank you for sharing a bit about yourself, though. That counts and takes courage. And we'll see if maybe we can work you into this class in the spring, if you want. We'll talk about it."

I sit down feeling a little warmer. A splash of hope in the Connecticut winter.

There's an awkwardly long silence as Miss Rishi's gaze swivels around the room, an expectant look on her face. She glances at her nails and then at all of us. Her eyebrows move up; she looks at her nails again. A few people squirm in their seats in front of me.

"Fine, I'll go," Frankie grumbles. She grabs her journal and walks up to the front of the class, and Miss Rishi walks toward me and, surprisingly, takes Frankie's seat. She glances over and smiles at me before looking ahead. A lot of the kids jostle out notebooks and pens, the sound of turning pages and scratching nibs filling the class.

"This is the part where you take notes, to share when she's done," Miss Rishi says, leaning across the little space between our desks.

"Oh!" I open up the new notebook and click my pen.

I'm ready, I guess.

"This piece is called 'Ironic,'" Frankie says, and then exhales. I feel swept up even before she speaks.

An old man turned ninety-eight.
He won the lottery and died the next day.
It's a black fly in your chardonnay.
It's a death row pardon two minutes too late.

And isn't it ironic?
Don't you think?

"Hold up," someone interrupts, and everyone glances over in the voice's direction. Some kid with thick black hair leans back in his chair, a pen in his hand. He's tapping it back and forth, like he's considering his point carefully. "Wait a second. That's *actually* not ironic."

"Right?" a girl with bright red hair next to him chimes in, a scowl on her face. I'm not sure what it is she's angry at. Who gets angry at a poem? "Considering the way irony is defined in Greek tragedy, I don't see how, like, a fly in your beverage applies."

Wow, I don't like these people.

"Yeah, that's not irony, that's just, like, shitty," the guy continues.

The redheaded girl nods, pointing at Frankie, and a couple kids in the class chuckle. I can't help but feel like this is less about the poem and more about her.

A bit of rage boils in my chest, but I push it back down. We had a kid like that in our writing group, once upon a time. Always bent on tearing everyone down as opposed to finding ways to critique while uplifting. That's how it's supposed to work. He didn't last long. Plus, everything he wrote was terrible. People who critique that way are often pretty bad.

"Can I please just finish my piece?" Frankie snaps, and looks toward the back of the class. Her eyes meet mine for a minute, and she tilts her head a little with a nod. And just like that, I think I understand what she meant by that

Thunderdome joke. Is it like this for everyone else in the class, though?

"Continue, Frankie," Miss Rishi says, waving her hand. "And remember, we share feedback and insight *after* pieces are finished."

The teacher glares at the backs of the students in front of me, and it genuinely feels intense enough that maybe they can feel it. Frankie clears her throat and continues.

Mr. Play-It-Safe was afraid to fly.
He packed his suitcase and kissed his kids goodbye.
He waited his whole damn life to take that flight.
And as the plane crashed down, he thought,
"Well, isn't this nice."
And isn't it ironic—

"It's not, though," someone else interrupts, and I can't help but groan. I glance over and it's some white kid on the other end of the room. A girl next to him is agreeing and nodding.

"Mike, I said—" Miss Rishi starts.

"It would be irony if the guy in the crash was, like, an airplane mechanic?" that girl interjects, and the dude, Mike, next to her nods vigorously. And I can't help but notice neither of them is actually talking to Frankie. They're chatting with each other about how wrong she is. There's no real conversation happening, no real critique. I don't think they're interested in helping her, and that pisses me off.

"Yeah, you're right," Mike continues. "Or if the guy was—"

"Oh my God." I slam my hand on my desk, and everyone turns around and looks at me. Frankie's eyes go a little wide, and then she snorts out a laugh. "How about all of you guys just let her finish?!"

I look over at Miss Rishi, who is staring at me with a wild look of amusement on her face.

"I'm . . . not sorry." I don't apologize and look back toward Frankie. "Please keep going. I, for one, love it."

Frankie smiles and flips to the next page.

· · ·

"Hey, wait up!"

I turn around as I'm hustling out of that classroom, the rest of my time in there a solid forty-five minutes of hell, listening to the rest of those pieces. Frankie's was amazing, but everyone else . . . I could have lived forever without listening to those hacks. Three of those terrible writers were students who called out Frankie during her "Ironic" poem, which, I suppose, is actually ironic.

I think?

Whatever. It doesn't matter. Who cares? Language is fluid, it's one of the first big lessons you learn in any writing class. Or, you know, from reading at least one book.

Frankie is holding her notebook to her chest, little sheets of paper sticking out of it, scrawled notes peeking at me. Her smile is outrageously gorgeous, and she runs her fingers along the side of her hair, tucking away a wayward curl.

"You didn't have to do that," she says, as someone pushes by her, knocking her notebook out of her hands. I bend down to help her pick it up, pieces of paper fluttering about. I snatch them out of the air and watch that first guy who called her out hurrying by, turning to look back at us just once.

"Hey—" I start, and move to get up.

Frankie grabs my arm, pulling me back.

"Come on," she says, tucking the rest of her poems into her notebook. "That douche is definitely not worth it."

But maybe you are.

I want to say that, but I absolutely don't. I don't even know this girl's last name yet. Ease up there, heart.

"They can't talk to you like that," I grumble, standing up with her. "Does that happen all the time? That's not how peer review and critiques should work."

"Yeah, well, racists don't care about getting feedback. They only like giving it."

"Damn." I laugh. "I can't argue that one."

"You're new here, so . . ." She hefts her tote bag up over her shoulder a little more. "You'll figure it out. Maybe in that class next year, if you take it and if you can *take* it, if you know what I mean. It's never about your writing with people like that. It's about your voice and how it scares them."

"Is that why you're in that class? You like scaring people?"

"Nah, I'm there because I like writing," she says, her smile tugging at the corner of her mouth. "But you know, there are perks." She looks down the hallway and back at me. "What's your next class?"

"Does it matter?" I ask. "I've got a week here before the break. Can I walk with you?"

"Depends." Her head tilts to the side, and she gives me a coy look that sends my heart racing yet again. "It'll cost you one poem."

"What?!" I laugh, but she just stares at me. "Oh, you're serious."

"Afraid I am, Phoenix." She grins, and then looks away, like we have all the time in the world in this hallway. I feel like if she had an apple, she'd lean against the lockers and take a bite out of it, like some sort of mastermind in a movie. "One poem, and you may escort me."

"I, um, didn't write anything," I stammer out.

"I know you've got a little notebook in your bag." She crosses her arms, her grin expanding. "Why don't you show me what you got?"

"Aren't you . . . we . . . going to be late for class?" I ask, trying to stall.

"It's the end of the year. Like you said, we'll all be on break soon, and no one even knows who you are yet." She shrugs. "I'm not worried about being marked late, and you shouldn't be worried about anything except getting me that poem."

She nods at my bag.

I look around, and the hallway is almost entirely empty, just a few students at the doorways to classrooms. I glance back at her.

"Well?" she asks.

I take a step toward the lockers, sigh, and dig around in my bag as I lean against the cool metal behind me. I pull out my weathered notebook, and she makes a satisfied "hmph" sound and I give her a playful glare. She laughs, and oh my God, that laugh. I cannot handle it.

I flip through to the piece Ruby left a note on.

"Okay." I hand her the notebook, and she steps back like I just tried to pass her a piece of rotten fruit. "What?!"

"Oh no, no." Frankie shakes her head. "You heard me read. It's your turn."

"No way!" I look around; the hallways are entirely empty now. "We're going to be—"

"I guess I'll walk to class alone."

"Fine, fine." I clear my throat and take another quick look around before beginning.

How 'bout me not blaming you for everything?
How 'bout me enjoying the moment for once?
How 'bout how good it feels to finally forgive you?
How 'bout grieving it all one at a time?
The moment I let go of it
Was the moment I got more than I could handle.
The moment I jumped off of it
Was the moment I touched down.

I glance up at Frankie, and she's staring at me, wide eyed.

"It's . . . not quite finished yet." I clear my throat again. "Does that get me a walk to your class?"

"Sure. Try to keep up," she says, taking off, and I hurry after her.

One thing's for sure.

I already don't know if it's possible to keep up with this Frankie girl.

But I think I'd really like to try.

Life has a funny way of sneaking up on you.

Mom: How was your first day?

Phoenix: It was . . . a day. Eventful. I liked that writing class.

Mom: Hang in there.

Mom: Meet anyone interesting? New friends?

Phoenix: Mom it doesn't work like that.

Phoenix: But kinda, I guess?

Phoenix: I might go to a party tomorrow night, if that's okay? Will you need me home?

Mom: No it's okay, I'm going to wrap up early at the practice and visit your sister.

Mom: Want me to FaceTime you?

Phoenix: I'll visit her tonight.

Phoenix: I'll head home first and get dinner prepped for you. In the mood for anything special?

Mom: You don't have to do that.

Mom: But your pasta with Alfredo sauce would be excellent.

Mom: But again you don't have to do that.

Mom: With chicken.

Phoenix: Hahah okay Mom.

Mom: Love you.

Nick: Hey, need me to bring anything tonight?

Nick: I can swing by earlier if you need some help moving shit around.

Andrew: I'm good, no worries. Lily's helping move stuff. That new substitute teacher is bringing the beer.

Nick: Hahah, what?!

Andrew: Hey, he wants to be cool. Let him. So no rush.

Andrew: And besides, me and Lily are having some us time before the party, if you know what I mean.

Andrew: You could bring your sister though.

Andrew: 😉

Nick: You're gross.

Nick: Knock it off.

Andrew: Just fucking with you man, chill.

Andrew: Is Bella coming? Did you man up and ask her?

Nick: She is. We talked about it at school.

Nick: And don't give me that man up shit. I'm taking my time. I don't want to mess things up.

Nick: I'm not like you. Bella's special.

Andrew: Right. If you don't make a move soon, I'm gonna.

Nick: Why are you such an asshole?

Nick: Oh, I invited that new kid.

Andrew: New kid?

Nick: Yeah, Phoenix something. He just started yesterday, we ended up having calculus together. Seems cool.

Andrew: I mean, that's okay, Mr. Welcoming Party.

Andrew: Just don't let him cramp my style.

Nick: You're insufferable. Fine.

Chapter Four

Nick

I hear them fighting before I open the front door.

I close my eyes, exhaling. The overly warm December day has faded with the afternoon, and I can see my breath, clouds of white against the eggshell-blue door to our house. I lean against it, my fist against the wood, and listen . . . quickly realizing the shouting is one-sided. It's just Mom, and she must be on the phone.

I'm so damn tired.

I have to be perfect. Flawless. A shining example in this disaster of a family, while they get to flip out on each other over breakfast and, now, on the phone. Me, I have to get the good grades, date the right people, get into the correct school, be this paragon, when all I want to do is cut class and maybe . . . I don't know, do anything else. Spend the day at the shitty empty mall in the next town over or hide in someone's basement playing video games. Just be like the rest of my friends. But that doesn't keep Mom holding it together. Letting myself cut loose only threatens to send her reeling.

Just half a year more. Six months. Then I'll be away and can be me, and not a parent to my parents. Six months to figure out how to not let the guilt of leaving overwhelm me and keep me rooted to the ground here. What happens when I go and leave Frankie behind with them? What happens to Dad and his quiet depression spiral? How long can he keep pretending, hiding in the dark only to explode when he's brought into the light just a little? What more will it take before he just walks out the door and never comes back?

I take a deep breath. Okay.

Time to put on my own show.

I open the front door, and Mom is standing there in the middle of the living room, her cheeks red, eyes watery. She looks furious but also . . . there's something else to it that I can't quite put my finger on. She looks sick, sweating the way you do when you're just getting over a fever, and she hangs up the phone, quickly tossing it onto the couch as she spots me.

"Hey . . ." I start, walking in slowly.

Her expression shifts quickly, a smile lighting up her face like someone just pasted it on there. She wipes at her cheeks and sniffles.

"What's, um . . . what's going on, Mom?"

"Hey, sweetheart," she says, her voice gone hoarse. "Nothing, it's nothing. Not feeling too great."

"Yeah, okay, well, it doesn't look like nothing," I press. "Do you want me to run out and get you anything? I can pick up some cold medicine or—"

"No, no." She shakes her head. "It's fine."

There's a beat, a little pause, interrupted by her sniffling.

"Was that Dad?" I ask, breaking the silence.

"Oh, I don't want you to worry about that," she says, waving her hand around. Which means it probably was Dad, and the likelihood of him coming home tonight has dropped by a significant percentage. He'll probably crash in his office and post a bunch of wildly depressing Instagram stories with quotes from bad songs about feeling alone, and I have no idea what I'm supposed to do when I see those.

"Was everyone just freaking out over you and Harvard at school?" she asks.

"No, not really." I shrug, and she frowns. I know she wants everyone around me to be celebrating and lifting me up on their shoulders or something, but every other day someone gets into a random school. The local county college, smaller state schools, places that all sound great but make Mom wince when she hears their names. No, there are just quiet nods and congrats, leaving someone else to stress over whether they'll be next to get a letter.

"I mean, some of my friends are hyped, I guess," I say. "I found out Shaune from down the block got into Berklee on early acceptance—"

"Isn't he that guitar kid who is always playing at the coffee shops?" she asks, squinting.

"Yeah." I nod. "He's pretty good, plays, like, emo stuff and acoustic pop covers. Anyway, I got invited to a party—"

"I don't know if it's a good idea for you to be hanging out with him." She shakes her head. "He seems like trouble."

"What?!" I laugh. "Trouble? Why? He plays Ed Sheeran covers and wears seashell necklaces. I'm not sure he could be less threatening."

"Still." She glances up toward the door and scratches at the back of her neck. "I heard he doesn't really study and got in just because he's good at music. According to Mrs. Niven down the block, his grades are just terrible."

"I don't . . ." I shake my head. "Didn't Mrs. Niven's kids graduate, like, five years ago? What does she even care?"

I don't have time for this. This careful unpacking of every single person she sees who stumbles into my orbit, whom I try to be friends with. Why is it bad to not do great in class, but excel somewhere else? The football players at our school sure as hell do it, and most of Mom's friends are sports parents. Or, like Mrs. Niven, they have kids who graduated ages ago, but for some reason still stay invested in our school or complain about the board of education on Facebook. Maybe I'll just talk with Shaune at school and online, maybe go on tour with his future band while skipping out on a semester or a year or, hell, all of college. I mean, I won't, because that sounds terrible, but the point is that I *could*.

Whew.

Six. Months. Left.

"Fine," I grumble.

"Did you want to do a movie tonight?" Mom asks, her tone shifting radically again from sour to sweet, like someone flicked a switch in her head. "There's that new Sarayu Blue movie on Netflix I know you wanted to watch."

I know how much Mom loves our movie nights. It used to be this wholesome family tradition, with all of us on the couch on Saturdays, that evolved from a bundle of family-friendly sitcoms to a full movie as Frankie and I got older. But these days, with the growing fissures between her and Dad and her and Frankie, it's just me keeping that routine alive. And really, that's been going on for longer than her and Dad's fights became things we could see, instead of just felt.

I could always tell when our parents were fighting or just had a shouting match, with the way they used to tip-toe around each other, force jokes or hugs. Now it all just happens in the open, with that routine following quickly after, making it feel even more fake.

But . . . there's Andrew's house party tonight, and it feels like it might be my last chance this year for a big blowout. And to potentially talk to Bella. Or, hell, any girl for that matter. Which is kind of hard to do when you're forced to be so laser focused on school, clubs, college, volunteering, being perfect perfect perfect while simultaneously trying to keep your crumbling family together.

Don't I deserve this? Just . . . a little something?

I hate trying to be perfect. I just want to be me.

"Maybe tomorrow night?" I venture, trying not to wince, bracing myself for her disappointment. "There's just . . . there's this party that Andrew is throwing, and it's sort of the year's last hurrah, you know?"

"Party?" she asks, tilting her head. "Do his parents know?"

"It's not *that* kind of party, Mom." I laugh a little but feel a swell of anxiety in my chest. Why not just lie completely? I didn't need to mention it was actually a party. Last thing I need is Mom calling up Andrew's family and tipping them off or using this as a gossip barb or jab in her group of terrible mother friends. "It's just a few people, grabbing pizza, playing video games, that sort of stuff."

I leave out all the talk about having a DJ and Andrew's claim that the young substitute teacher everyone is crushing on is swinging by with a keg and alcohol. That it's less about pizza and more about drinking, and the only games people will be playing likely have to do with making out during heated truth-or-dare tournaments where no one ever picks truth.

No one wants truth.

"I don't know . . ." Mom wrings her hands a little. "I'm not sure you should go."

"Come on, Mom," I huff. "I won't stay too late, and besides, who else is going to keep an eye on everyone?"

Which isn't a lie. That's my role at almost every single party I go to, whether it's a holiday party with extended family and I'm keeping an eye on just how much beer Dad is sneaking on outdoor patios with his brothers, or I'm babysitting everyone at a parentless throwdown at someone's mansion, holding on to car keys. I don't necessarily mind it, keeping my friends safe. Being that guy who isn't drinking.

But I know once I leave this suburb, it'll be different.

Maybe I'll make friends who want to watch out for me for once.

I'd like to try at least one Jell-O shot before I die.

"Okay." Mom softens. "But be home before midnight, and if your sister shows up, keep an eye on her."

I snort out a laugh, and she looks at me seriously.

"For real?" I scoff. "Mom, there's no way she's going to one of Andrew's get-togethers. The Montefiores are not her kind of people."

"Well, you never know." She sighs. "I feel like I overheard her talking about some kind of party with Jo. She's been lashing out so much lately, I wouldn't be surprised if I came home and she was here, tangled up in some shocking party with all her friends."

"Eh, yeah. I don't know about that," I say. The idea of Frankie being able to say something like "all her friends" and have it not just mean Jo and, like, I don't know, any of those kids she writes with sometimes is pretty laughable. She has her small band, I've got my big social circle, and God, what I wouldn't do to trade places there.

When your circle is smaller, people see you.

When it's wide and all encompassing? You get lost on the edges.

Mom flops down on the couch and lazily reaches for the television remote.

"Just . . . you be careful, okay?" She looks off at the television.

"I will, I will." I make my way toward the stairs and my

room to get myself ready. Maybe a new outfit, some of that cologne I know poor Frankie hates. Tonight's the night, though. I'll talk to Bella. We'll make the most of these last few months. Something, anything.

I bound up the stairs and hear some music coming from Frankie's room. I edge closer to the door, Paramore booming through her computer speakers. I think about knocking but stop myself. She's still upset with me. Best to just let her cool—

I hear a loud snore.

I squint, listening, but it's not coming from Frankie's room. I walk back to the landing and peer over the banister, and Mom is already passed out, her arm over her head, the television remote dangling from her hand. I walk back down and glance into the kitchen. There's a half-drained bottle of wine on the counter, an empty, freshly used wineglass on the countertop. Dad will see this and it'll be a whole thing, so I tiptoe my way in and toss the glass in the dishwasher, cork the bottle, and put it back in the fridge.

I close the big stainless steel refrigerator and press my head against the cold surface. I deserve this one night, just one night to be less than perfect. I can leave for the night, but I don't know about college. How can I walk away from all this?

Half a bottle of wine and melting down in the living room.

When it's barely 4:00 P.M.

There's some spilled wine on the marble countertop, and I grab a rag to wipe it up . . . and spot Mom's pain medicine sitting on the edge of the sink, open. I suck at my teeth and remember the open, half-downed bottle of wine.

That's got to be an accident, right? She wouldn't mix pain meds and liquor, she's too smart. Too much of a helicopter around me and Frankie. She *shouldn't* be mixing her meds with her drinks; it doesn't matter how much it might make the pain hurt a little bit less. I cap the meds, which are nearly empty, and look at the side of the bottle. It says she was due for a refill nearly several months ago. I guess she doesn't really need them anymore. Good.

I put the pills on a little shelf by the sink. I make my way back into the living room and grab one of the many throw blankets she's collected and draped over just about every piece of furniture in the house. I unfurl it and tuck her in on the couch before heading back upstairs to get ready.

She lets out another snore, and unease swirls in my chest as I ascend the staircase.

And I wonder . . .

. . . if the helicopter is about to crash.

Nick: Hey dad, are you on your way home?

Dad: Yup, on the train. Should be there in 20.

Nick: Can you keep an eye on mom tonight?

Dad: Oh, sure, why?

Nick: I don't know, I think she maybe had a bit too much wine right after taking her pain meds.

Dad: Goddamn it.

Dad: You shouldn't have to see that.

Nick: It's fine, people make mistakes.

Nick: Just wanted you to make sure she's okay.

Nick: Maybe watch a movie? She's snoozing on the couch. I'm going to a party tonight, otherwise I'd stay home and do the same.

Dad: Fine, fine.

Dad: Your sister texted me and said she's heading to that party at Andrew's. I'll keep an eye on Mom if you keep an eye on her.

Nick: Ugh, okay.

Dad: Sorry champ. That's being a man for you. Watch out for the people around you. It's less about you, and more about them.

Nick: Right. I seem to recall you being a little upset about having to watch mom.

Dad: Hey that's not why I'm upset.

Dad: It's the meds and the drinking.

Dad: Sigh. I'm sorry. You're right.

Dad: You're a good kid, Nick.

Dad: Stay out of trouble.

Chapter Five

Bella

I hug my leather jacket close to me as I walk toward Andrew's house, passing by a series of carbon copy homes that would look glamorous if they didn't all look exactly the same. Everything about his street—and the neighborhood—is that way. Streetlamps all spaced the same distance. Lawns maintained in a similar fashion, looking like they're all fake grass on the high school football field. Even the oak trees feel off, all still too young, not really ready to be called an "oak" yet.

The Connecticut winter breeze slaps against my cheeks, and my eyes start to water a little. Why am I even going to this? I don't even particularly *like* Andrew, I just tolerate him because he's always around Nick. But Mom and Dad are all about his family, the Montefiores, the only family in town that has a last name that sounds like it belongs on a five-dollar bottle of wine that's labeled a "full-bodied white" or something.

A convertible zooms down the street, the roof down, people inside screaming along to a pop song I don't recognize. It's freezing out, but I suspect they're still feeling warm inside that car. I pick up my pace, passing lawn after lawn, same driveway after same driveway, until Andrew's house starts to stick out among the clones. It's easy to see, considering all the cars parked around it. His driveway is full, there are cars on both sides of the street, bikes strewn about the sidewalks. A few electric scooters are sitting near the steps to the front door, just begging someone to steal them.

It's all just a big red flag saying "party over here," and I already know it's only a matter of time before it gets busted and shut down.

Someone standing on Andrew's steps waves to me, shouting my name over the muted thumping music that's clearly got to be booming on the inside. I can't imagine I'll hang around for long, but hopefully in the throngs of all these people I can at least get a few good drinks and find some time to chat with Nick.

I pull out my phone, the screen lighting up the dark sidewalk.

Nick: See you there?

Me: You bet.

Nick: ♥

Oh. Oh, that heart.

Maybe this is it. Maybe we'll finally talk about whatever has been bubbling up between the two of us this last . . . God, I don't even know. Entire year? Sure, he's off to Harvard, and I'm moving to New York for school, but it's not like Boston and New York City are some impossible distance from each other. Trains exist, and I've always loved those long rides from Hartford up to Providence in the autumn with my family to visit Mom's side. Watching all the foliage go by from the observation car, the terrible train food, luscious naps as the sun poured in through large glass windows . . .

There was this old punk song Dad used to listen to . . . "Amtrak Is for Lovers." He'd bring it up whenever we were going to take one of those trips, and Mom would laugh about it, how he'd make the same reference every single time.

I've been spinning it a lot lately. We haven't done one of those family trips in a while, but the two of them keep talking about taking one the summer after graduation, maybe all the way across the country on the rails. That song, though. It's weirdly about breaking up, so I'm not quite sure why Mom and Dad listen to it or reference it. I think maybe they only like the title.

I do too.

I look around at the bikes and the cars, trying to spot Nick's ride in the double-parked, half-on-the-curb mayhem.

"Amtrak Is for Lovers." Hm.

One can dream.

• • •

I swear, the inside of Andrew's house is so hot it feels like his walls are about to start sweating. Is that a thing? I consider taking my jacket off the second I step inside, but think better of it when I see a large pile of them on what might be a shoe rack, several not-quite-empty cans of White Claw carelessly thrown on top of the coats. There's a significant amount of hard seltzer all over the top layers, and I just pull my leather jacket closer to me, despite the heat. I'll take being a little sweaty over being sticky with raspberry seltzer, thanks.

Andrew's lavish living room is just packed full of people from school and . . . definitely some kids who aren't quite kids anymore. There's got to be a bundle of college students here; there are just too many full beards that don't look like they belong in a high school. It's like the cast of *Riverdale* in here, where you just *know* that background extra is pushing close to thirty.

And drinks are just everywhere. Not only the spilled ones on the jackets, but just open coolers and large metal containers that look like they're made for indoor plants, overflowing with cans and bottles. There's a couple making out on the couch, despite everyone standing around them, and I'm pretty sure it's Jeff and Ramie from band. At least they're adorable. I'm not sure if our yearbook has a Best Couple category, but if it does, those two will claim that title in a heartbeat.

All these kids and near-adults, but I don't see Andrew, Lily, or—

A guy stumbles out of the kitchen into the living room, holding Julia Stone's hand, the two of them giggling. I know her only from a handful of classes we've had together, and I wouldn't say we're friends or anything. He keeps glancing back at her, a smile on his stubbled face, and her bright green eyes are full of coy mischief.

It's the guy she's with that gives me pause.

He's way older, and when I finally get a good look at him, I realize he's the substitute teacher Andrew said was getting us the beer. He's been covering for Mr. Garcia, who saved up an ungodly amount of personal days to take a two-week-long cruise and made sure students knew that's what he was doing. It felt like every class that got closer to his trip, we focused less on Spanish lessons and more on the places he was planning to visit while he was away. Good for him.

But hell no am I letting *this* happen.

I storm over, nearly colliding with the teacher as he gets close to the stairway that heads up toward the second floor—and the bedrooms.

"Hey, careful," he mutters, smirking, and tries to nudge by me.

"Come on, Julia." I reach out, putting myself in between the two of them. She shirks away a little. "Julia," I press, talking between gritted teeth.

"Get lost, Bella." She laughs, playfully trying to swat me away. "Mr. Alden is hot."

"Don't be a buzzkill," Mr. Alden says, and up until now, I barely remembered his last name. He was just that substitute teacher I never had but everyone muttered about. *Oh, he's so cool, so funny, so sexy . . .*

I can't help myself. I shove him.

"Hey!" he grumbles, blinking. "What are you—"

"Get out," I snap. I feel the vibe in the room shift. Some people have stopped talking; there's an audible sound of feet moving and bodies turning. Someone snorts out a laugh, and I hear the *pssst* of a beer bottle opening over the music.

"No way, I brought the beer. I'm—" he starts, and I pull out my phone, waving it in my hand.

"Do I need to shoot a video or something? Pictures?" I glance back at everyone in the room, and dozens of heads turn away. A couple of the older college kids look visibly uncomfortable, and I wonder if they know him. "How will that look? In fact, hold on, let me just—" I hold the phone up.

"Okay, damn," he says, holding an arm up to block his face while simultaneously swinging his other one at my phone. How he didn't think of this possibility before coming here with beer and plans to get with a student, I don't know. "I'm out, be cool. Be cool."

He hustles out of the living room, fumbles for his jacket in the pile of White Claw–soaked coats, and is out the door in seconds. A few of the college kids quickly follow him, mumbling to one another, protecting their faces with their hands, and my suspicions were spot on. Creeps. I shove my phone back in my pocket, and Julia is still there, glaring at me.

"I can't believe you messed that up for me." She scowls, crossing her arms and looking back toward the rest of the party. "Like, half the older guys just left. Way to go."

"I saved you," I scoff, shaking my head. "He's a gross old man. You'll thank me tomorrow when you're sober."

"Whatever." She stomps off back toward the kitchen, and I lean against the staircase's banister. The party goes back to the previous volume like nothing happened. Like a teacher wasn't just about to try to sleep with a student and a gaggle of creepy older college kids wasn't here, likely with the same exact motives. But that's how it is in this town. Shit happens all the time, but it's easier to just move on.

I might as well too.

I make my way to the kitchen, following Julia's path. A few shoulders bump against me, hot breath and hair tickling my neck as I squeeze by. I burst through the last group of partygoers and inch my way into the kitchen, where I finally find Andrew. He throws his hands up in the air in victory over sinking a beer pong ball, and I can't help but laugh at the pair up against him on the other side, Helen and Chris, two kids in my calculus class with Miss Vicente. They both wince as they chug back whatever is in those red cups.

Andrew high-fives his partner, and when she steps forward, I realize it's Lily, one of his best friends and maybe girlfriend? I'm never quite sure what the deal is with those two. But I suppose that's a popular theme when it comes to the people I surround myself with, like with Nick's sister, Frankie, and her maybe-girlfriend, Jo. They can try to be as sneaky and secretive as they want around school, but I see right through them. I only wish it were easier for them both. I'm not sure how Frankie's parents would take her being out, and I already know how Jo's deal with her. We're not close, but I've overheard more than enough since freshman year. It sucks.

Andrew's eyes catch mine, and a smile erupts on his face. He grabs a White Claw and strolls over, and when I shake my head at it, he swaps it for a beer on the kitchen counter. I smile, and he pops it open on the hard surface and hands it to me. He looks like he actually put a little effort into his appearance today for once. He's always just-got-out-of-bed or recently-ran-a-mile chic, a bit bedraggled but still handsome despite what a smug prick he can be. Lily could do way better—I'm not sure why she carries on with him.

"Cheers." He grins, toasting my bottle with his red cup. It's some kind of wheat beer and tastes like a piece of bread from an organic grocery store. Not sure if that's a good thing or not. "I'm glad you're here."

"Wouldn't miss it." I take another sip of bread and survey the kitchen. It's not as wildly packed as the living room, which is a surprise, as kitchens are generally the gathering point for most parties. There are a few people leaning against the counter, a handful fussing over beer pong, but it's not bad. Might just stay in here the rest of this thing.

There's some movement by the door leading into the

living room, and Nick strolls in with Frankie. He spots me almost immediately and takes a few strides over, and I can see Andrew's expression darken for just a minute before he lightens back up again. I know Andrew's got this silly crush on me, and has for years, but he's with Lily. Kinda. And besides, I'm just not interested.

It's been Nick for me, all year. Probably longer, if I'm honest with myself.

"Hey," Nick says, a little smirk on his face, not quite able to look me in the eyes. God, he's so damn cute when he softens up like that, like a freshly baked cinnamon roll.

"Hey, yourself." I smirk back, and glance over at Frankie, who catches up and joins our little group. "I'm surprised you came, Frankie!"

"Same, honestly." Nick shrugs. "We ran into each other walking over here."

"Oh?" I ask.

"Yeah, I . . ." Frankie huffs. "Nick, I'm . . . you know, yesterday Mom was just being so awful, and I kinda lost it on you a bit. Sorry. Thought maybe this would make up for it."

"Meeting up with me at a party?" Nick asks, though he's smiling. "And not answering my texts about it?"

"No." Frankie mischievously grins and reaches into her dark blue leather jacket. She pulls out a bottle of cheap rum. I don't know rum, but it's in a plastic bottle, and I feel like that's a pretty clear sign of cheapness. She holds it by the cap and waves it around like she's ringing a bell.

"Where did you—" Nick starts.

"Dad has a stash in his den." She lets go of the bottle. Nick just barely catches it, but it's not like it would matter, plastic bottle and all. "He's not going to miss a six-dollar bottle of . . ." She squints at it as Nick holds it up. "First Lieutenant Morgan? What is that, a grade under captain?"

"That seems like copyright infringement," Andrew says, looking at the bottle.

"Well, here's hoping it tastes fine." Frankie laughs.

"Thanks," Nick says, looking at the bottle in his palm.

"You don't have to be perfect, you know," Frankie says, and this conversation is starting to feel a bit . . . like something they should have had outside before coming in here. "Just be you."

"Shots?!" someone's voice blares next to me. I startle back, and it's Lily with a tray of tiny red cups, some kind of clear liquid with little splashes of yellow, orange, and red swirling around inside them, almost like tiny fish. Weird-looking drinks or not, I'm happy for the interruption; things were getting a bit too personal over here. I squint at the cups and Lily grins.

"Goldfish shots," she says, and then whispers, "Not made of real goldfish, I swear."

Everyone reaches out for one, and I watch Nick and Frankie toast theirs, before we all down them at once. Frankie's entire face crumples in like a star collapsing in on itself. Nick coughs and covers his mouth, and some tears trickle down my face. It might as well have been real goldfish, because whatever liquor was in it would have certainly killed anything swimming in there.

"Want another?" Andrew asks me, and I shake my head.

"No way, those things are—"

"Round two!" Lily shouts, and another tray practically materializes in front of her. Nick and Frankie scowl at the tray, and only Nick reaches out for one, so slowly that it's hilarious.

"Come on, drink up," Andrew says, nudging me. He hands me a shot, and I wince, shooting it back. I smack my lips and wipe my mouth.

"That's gonna be a wrap for me." I laugh, coughing a little.

"No way, it's a party!" Andrew exclaims, and throws his arm around me, squeezing me into a side hug. I cringe, and he lets go, ducking away. "I'm gonna get some more!" he shouts, and disappears from our circle.

"Yeah, well, I'm definitely done," Frankie says, looking around. Her eyes light up as she looks back toward the living room. "You came!"

I squint, and in walks Phoenix, a new kid who appeared as randomly as that tray of shots at our school. He's cute, has this whole Latinx indie rocker/beat poet vibe going for him, his hair fluffed up in a wave, a thick corduroy jacket over skintight jeans. His look says "I have an acoustic guitar in my car and maybe a poetry chapbook in my pocket," and it works for him.

"I'm here." He smiles and nods at Nick, looking a bit awkward. He'll definitely be that kid who breaks the ice with a cover of a Shawn Mendes song when he heads off to college, but he'll actually pull it off instead of appearing like a douchebag. I can see it.

"I'm glad but . . . not really feeling this party," Frankie says, reaching out and tugging on his jacket. "What do you think, Nick?"

"I don't know." Nick looks over at me, smiling. "I'd like to see where it goes."

I'm trying to fight the blush that's heating up my cheeks, and I catch Frankie rolling her eyes, a little smile on her face.

"Well, I think I saw someone mixing cough medicine and rum out there, so I'm not sure this place is for me much longer," Phoenix says just as Andrew returns, cups in hand.

"Don't be silly." Andrew laughs, handing cups out to all of us. I cautiously take mine and give it a sniff. I glance up at Nick, who takes a sip of his drink.

"You want to get out of here?" Phoenix asks, looking at Frankie.

"Absolutely," she says.

Frankie looks at Nick, who nods at the door. "If Dad asks, I'll tell him you're still with me," he says, a soft smile on his face.

"You're the best," Frankie says, bouncing away from Phoenix to give her brother a hug. "See you at home."

"Yeah, you'd better." Nick glances over at Phoenix, who promptly looks around self-consciously.

It's funny and awkward, but . . . I thought . . . Frankie and Jo were a thing?

What is this?

Oh well, not my problem. That's this town, right? See the drama, see the bubbling-up problem, and turn away. Mind your business, keep your head low. You don't get in trouble that way; no one gossips about you if you stay out of things and avoid making yourself the center of attention.

"Oh, Nick!" Lily exclaims, digging around in her pockets. "Is that shot going to be it for you? Because I've got my keys, and a few of the other people playing drove and—"

"You know what?" Nick says, and looks over at me, grinning. He grabs a second shot off the tray and downs it, coughing immediately after. He clears his throat, tears pricking at his eyes. "Okay, no more of those, but . . . I'm not collecting keys tonight. I'm having some fun for once."

I reach out and grab another shot off the tray, and Andrew toasts his shot to the sky, wrapping his arm around Nick.

"Yeah!" Andrew shouts. "The party begins!"

Cheers.

Mom: Your sister sends her hellos.

Mom: [load attached media]

Phoenix: Aw, she looks great.

Phoenix: Was today . . . a good day?

Mom: Pretty good. She's eating and drinking okay, pain is manageable.

Mom: Dinner was delicious, thank you, by the way.

Phoenix: No problem.

Mom: The party going alright?

Phoenix: It's fine. I'll probably be home a little sooner than expected.

Phoenix: Bit too wild for me, going for a walk with some friends.

Mom: Some friends.

Mom: I like that.

Mom: Be safe.

Phoenix: Hey, sorry I didn't come by tonight with mom.

Ruby: It's fine, she reloaded my iTunes and I already bought the new season of Trillions.

Phoenix: Oh my God why don't you just stream that stuff?

Ruby: One, I want to support artists.

Ruby: Two, the Wi-Fi in this hospital is terrible. The faster I download stuff while it's working, the more likely I'll just have it to watch whenever.

Phoenix: I don't know what it is with you and those shows.

Ruby: Hey, "rich white people treating each other terribly" is my favorite genre.

Phoenix: Hahah, fine fine.

Phoenix: Still, sorry I wasn't there. I'll make it up to you.

Ruby: Make it up to me by having a blast tonight and the rest of this week.

Ruby: Do a bit of living for me and all that, you know?

Phoenix: Ugh, I hate when you say that.

Ruby: I know. ♥

Chapter Six

Frankie

I hug my leather jacket close to me as Poston Park, a small patch of woods with a field and a playground near Andrew's house, slowly comes into view. The modest mansions and sprawling driveways, the matching streetlamps and uniform trees, part ways for the last remaining holdout of nature in the suburban sprawl. The tips of the old pine trees peak into the sky like arrows, rising above us as we stroll up a hill.

"Oh, wow," Phoenix says once we reach the top, the final crest revealing the woods. He's been texting while we've walked on and off, the light from his phone illuminating his face. A large, elaborately painted sign with letters that look like they belong on a coffee shop blackboard or a fancy illustrated journal, reading POSTON PARK, sits at the entrance, a dirt path leading into the dark canopy. A catalog of don't-do-this, don't-do-that is posted alongside it. No drinking, no open flames, no ATVs . . . a list of exciting suggestions that no one likely even thinks of until they see the sign telling them not to do any of it.

I take my phone out, thinking of maybe lighting up the path with the flashlight, but it's not too dark. The moon is bright enough, and the streetlamps that border the woods cast a light glow through the trees. Phoenix is staring at the sign and peering up at the canopy.

"Have you not seen the park yet?" I ask.

"No. Not really." His eyes are wide in the dark. "I think we drove by here once or twice, but I didn't realize it was, like, a proper wilderness."

"Well, you're not gonna find any deer in there." I snort out a laugh. "Raccoons and chipmunks, mostly."

"Still." He gazes up toward the sky. "Pretty cool. Beautiful, even." He looks back down at me, smiling, and I can feel the heat rising to my cheeks.

"Yeah, well." I clear my throat and nod toward the path. "Come on, there's a playground and a big field at the end of this."

He hurries over and we walk into the woods. He stumbles a little on the dirt path, looking back down at his phone.

"Careful," I say, scratching my foot against the ground. "It's not exactly paved."

"Yeah, I noticed that." He laughs and then shivers a little. "Wow, it's, like, wildly cold out here. You okay?"

"I'll be fine." For all the crap Mom gave me about dressing warmer and not as "provocative" or whatever, I'm doing pretty all right out here. The combination of my sweater and jacket has me feeling toasty, but Phoenix's corduroy jacket doesn't seem to be doing him many favors. "Are you?"

"Oh, I'll tough it out." He grins, glancing at me. The shadowed canopy stretches for a beat, just like the quiet between the two of us, but much like the atmosphere around us, it feels natural. Nice. Generally, in my home, silence means something is wrong. At least when my parents are shouting at each other, it's like they are *attempting* to fix things. But when they walk around the house shrouded in quiet, a blend of sharp head turns and loud exhales, there's a near-violent quality to the hush.

I remember last year when Nick got a B- in some class that didn't matter—it might have even been gym—and Mom opted to give him the silent treatment for nearly a week. It drove him nuts, and I swear, I could hear him grinding his teeth through the wall between our rooms. She rambled about how his status at the top of his class was at risk, how could he get such a bad grade in such a simple class. She still brings it up sometimes, with him "only" being in the running to be salutatorian and not valedictorian.

Oh, Nick. I genuinely hope he has some fun tonight.

But this quiet . . . this kind of quiet is different. With a boy who smells like sandalwood and sends a blush screaming to my cheeks . . . this I like.

Though I don't know how Jo would feel about this.

We're not anything official; we haven't even really talked about it. We're just . . . best friends who make out

84

and fool around and sleep together when our parents aren't home sometimes? But even just thinking that, I know I'm lying to myself, and I should probably not be enjoying this moment in the pines with Phoenix as much as I am.

His fingertips brush against my hand, and he shirks away.

"Oh, sorry," he says, a little breathless, like he'd thrown everything into that attempt and lost his nerve, like a runner taking off at the start of a race and deciding he wants to take a walk instead.

"It's okay." I let out a little laugh, a plume of cold air visible in front of me. That Connecticut winter is sneaking up on us, a drastic change from this morning. I debate reaching out and grabbing his hand myself, but then I think better of it. There's Jo, still in the back of my mind. And I only just met him.

But still . . . sometimes that's all you need. A day. A moment. To feel and know something is there. And I just so desperately want to feel something, I don't know, new. In the wake of everything with Mom, Dad, Nick . . . just something *else* that isn't this constant soul suck.

The end of the dirt path opens up to a large field, tucked away and hidden by the tall pine trees, and the air smells of the sharp, cold pine needles. The frozen grass crunches as we make our way across it. A couple of winter fireflies dart about in the chill, their lights soft and faded, and it makes me sad, thinking of how they're still out here, doomed and looking for love.

Like the rest of us.

"Wow," Phoenix murmurs, turning to look at the playground at the other end of the field. He stops walking and gazes at me, a mischievous smirk on his face.

"What?" I ask, searching his smile for an answer.

"Race you!"

And he takes off running across the field.

I run after him, the crisp air slicing my cheeks like paper cuts, the dew-frozen grass sliding under my feet, threatening to send me reeling. I start to get a bit closer, and he turns for just a second, still flashing that smirk, and picks up a bit of speed, reaching the playground before me. He spins around, his arms out, looking so wildly satisfied with himself. I stop running and stroll the rest of the way there, and he cocks his head to the side, his expression impatient.

"Nice of you to join me." He grins.

"You move fast."

"I hope that's okay." His grin gets a little bigger, and I laugh, swatting at him. This boy. This boy is trouble, and I feel like he knows it. Which makes all this even worse. He carries all that charming danger like it's part of his corduroy jacket, slung over his shoulders and just effortlessly there. And he absolutely sees it.

What must that feel like, walking through this world, feeling seen and knowing it?

I know Mom and Dad and Nick see me. I'm there. I'm not invisible. But even so, it doesn't feel like they properly *see* me. Instead it's more like . . . there are waves of heat in front of me on a summer day, making me blurry. I'm there,

I'm present, but they aren't catching any of the details. I'm different from them. I stand out in our family, and I wish instead of trying to fit me into the puzzle of their little suburban life, they'd recognize I need to stand out. Be my own person. That no matter how much Mom tries, I'm not going to be the blue-eyed, blond-haired white girl she wanted.

He walks over to a swing set and plops down on one of the swings, the chains rattling above him. The whole playground consists of equipment that, despite the opulence of the neighborhood, feels dated and dingy. I suppose that's the plight of a playground in a town where everyone can fit their own in their yards. The paint on the swing set is faded and chipped away, silver metal glimmering through flakes of blue, and the playground itself has seen better days: slides with bits of graffiti, plastic explorable tubes that look like they've been wailed on by too many Wiffle ball bats, discarded cans and cheap beer bottles tucked away in the mulch surrounding it all.

Though I suppose all the signs of wear and tear are signs of being loved.

There are memories here, etched in the plastic, dug into the dirt, by hands big and small.

And I wonder what it is I'll leave behind, when it's finally my turn to say goodbye to places like this.

"So . . ." Phoenix says, as I sit next to him on the other swing. He pushes off the ground, his feet kicking the wood chips beneath him, the chains squeaking loudly. "Tell me your life story."

I laugh, and his smile whooshes by me as he swings.

"I'm serious," he says, digging his feet into the mulch as he comes back down, stopping. "What's your deal? Someone who writes the way you do . . . you've got to have lived a life that makes you want to tell a story. So. What is it?"

"I'm . . . not sure I've lived a story worth telling yet." I laugh, twisting in the swing a little, the chains grinding together. "I'm trying, though. My life isn't a finished novel."

"Then read me the rough draft."

Damn, Phoenix. I don't even know what to say to that, so I just exhale, thinking.

"I mean, okay, to start, what's the deal with your brother?" he asks, and with the way his eyes quickly look me over as he says it, I can feel the question coming. "Do you guys have . . . different . . ." He winces. "Okay, maybe I have no idea how to talk about that without sounding wildly rude or invasive."

"I know what you're trying to ask." I sigh. "It's fine. I'm adopted."

"Oh!" he exclaims, taken aback. "I was kinda leaning toward separated parents or a blended family . . ." He glances up toward the field. "My dad left my mom not too long ago, when my sister started getting really sick, and my mind just kind of wanders there. To separating and divorce and all that fun stuff."

"Sick?" I ask.

"Yeah. That's why we're here." He looks at me, his expression a bit harder. "Turns out the hospital here in

Greenport has the best facility for her, way better than back at home. I mean, there are good hospitals there, I'm not hating on my town, but . . . I don't know. You know how you see commercials for, like, hospitals and institutions saying they have the best treatment in the country for this and that?"

"Sure." I shrug.

"Well, this place is like that. They have those ads on television and at train stations and on billboards, like that's what you want to think about while traveling." He wrings his hands together and cracks his knuckles. "Anyway. It's kind of a long-term treatment deal, so here we are."

It's hard not to notice that he hasn't said just what it is his sister has, and I wonder if it's one of those words you don't say out loud. Like it gives it power or something, speaking whatever it is. When Mom's oldest sister passed years ago, when Nick and I were in junior high, it was from cancer. And you just didn't say the word around the house.

But that's also my mom. The silent treatment whenever she's upset about something or at someone. As though not talking is going to make it wither away. When in reality, her silent treatment when she's upset at me or Nick only makes *us* wither. I think sometimes being quiet about something only makes it stronger. Builds resentment.

"So, is that your story?" I ask.

"Some of it, though it's mostly my sister's story," he says. "Though when someone else's story is that major a part of your life, it kinda becomes your story. Like you're the side character."

"Oof." I puff out my cheeks and exhale.

"What?"

"It's just . . ." I sigh. "I get that. I mean, no one in my family is sick like that. It's not"—I groan—"I don't know, dire. I'm not sure how to talk about it without being insensitive."

"No, it's okay," he presses. "Go on."

"But you asked about my brother, right? He's this . . . beacon of all that is good in my mom's eyes, and I think my dad's too, to some extent, though he doesn't quite stress over it the way my mom does. Everything he does is perfect, and if it isn't, they push him to be. So, the spotlight is always just zeroed in on him, and I'm off on the side, singing in the chorus."

"How does he feel about that?" Phoenix asks.

I blink for a minute, looking down at the grass on the dark field.

"I'm not sure." I clear my throat. "It's one of those things we don't quite talk about."

"Is there a lot your family just doesn't talk about?"

For a second, I almost hold back my laugh, but it's just him and this open field and the trees, so I let loose. I shake my head and grin at him.

"Plenty." I chuckle. "We never talk about me being the adopted one. No one in my family does, even though when I walk in a room for a holiday get-together and a cousin has a new boyfriend or someone's brought a pal from work, their eyes zip right to me. Like, who is this random Black kid? I'm convinced my mom or dad takes these people into a bathroom or a hallway and whispers my story to them, to try to stop the awkward looks from across the room, but who knows. It's just this . . . elephant in the room, you know? My mom couldn't get pregnant again, not after Nick, so I was brought into the picture."

"Do you think your insecurity about your family life has to do with why you're insecure about your writing?" he asks.

I stare at him. "Who *are* you?" I ask, laughing a little.

"My mom is a child psychologist," he says. "It's why we can afford to be here, for Ruby's treatments, even if just barely. Definitely just barely."

"I guess that explains why you're good at asking questions like that." I try not to scowl and look down into my hands. "But yeah, maybe. My parents aren't super into the writing stuff. Well, Mom isn't. Dad doesn't say much."

"That seems like a bit of a theme."

"He tries." I sigh. "My mom's a bit overbearing. Takes the focus. That spotlight I was just talking about. Plus, he's always at work. There's only so much he can do, I think. And work is the one place where he can get away from her."

"Well, don't let them get in the way of your dreams."

He gets up off the swing and walks around the swing set, cupping his hand around a metal bar and spinning around it. He smiles and walks over to me and gives me a little push on the swing. I close my eyes for a second, feeling the breeze in my hair, as I whoosh up and down, back and forth, mirroring the way my heart is feeling during this deep conversation.

"I get all of it, though," he says, and with each little push, my shoulders are waiting for his hands to come back and press against them. "I love my family. My mom tries her best, my sister is a fighter. My dad is an asshole who left us when things got a little too hard and is currently on the West Coast dating someone half his age. It's pretty unfair for him to chase joy and happiness at the expense of, you know, us. But what can you do?"

"Do you ever wish you had another family?" I ask.

I swing back, and this time, his hands catch me, slowing me down until I'm swaying softly in front of him. He swings around the steel bar of the frame near us and leans against it, looking right at me.

"I don't know about different," he says. "I wonder if *I* were different if my dad might call more, you know? If there was something I could have done to get him to stay around, support my mom, support Ruby's fight."

"Yeah, I hear you." I nod. "I sometimes feel like if I were different my mom might really love me."

His eyes flit up to mine, urgent. "She loves you," he insists.

"Yeah, I don't know, you haven't met her." I look away. "She loves Nick. Falls to pieces over every little thing he does. I read an essay online once about how squeaky wheels get the oil, in families and most relationships. Friendships, whatever. But in my family's case, the good wheel gets all the oil, and the squeaky one is left to fall off and roll down the road."

Phoenix sputters out a laugh. "That's how a car crash happens," he says.

"Yeah, well." I sniffle. "I already feel like a wreck."

"That's not what I see," he says, taking a step away from the pole, standing in front of me. He bites his lower lip, and I swallow, my throat going dry. Goodness.

"What . . . do you see?" I ask.

He squints at me a little and smiles sheepishly in a way that leaves a dimple cratering his cheek.

"Do you have a boyfriend?" He cocks his head to the side. "You *have* to have a boyfriend. Someone you take to parks like this and have deep conversations with and make embarrassing but sweet Spotify playlists for."

Jo flashes through my mind, and my breath goes short.

"I . . . I don't," I say, not entirely lying. I don't have a boyfriend. I have . . . a best friend who's maybe something, but I'm not sure. If she was something, she'd be a girlfriend. So . . .

Not lying?

These are some . . . mental gymnastics, that's for sure.

He runs his hands through his hair and smirks at me again. "All right. Good to know."

"And what about you?" I ask, hopping off the swing. "What's your deal? I saw you texting while we strolled over here. Girlfriend back home?"

"Oh, no, definitely not." He laughs. "Just checking in with my mom and Ruby. I, uh, usually visit most nights and took today off to . . . well, here we are. Prepped dinner for my mom too, which is also a semi-daily thing. Thankfully she has a weakness for fast food, because I can't cook every single day."

He grins, like everything he just said isn't wildly devastating. Almost every night with his sister at the hospital, makes dinner for his mom after work . . . when does he have time to do, like, stuff for himself? He must see my expression sour because he shrugs.

"It is what it is," he says. "It's all a bit uninvited, I know. But my sister, she didn't ask to get sick, and my mom didn't ask for all this to fall on her shoulders. Least I can do is lighten the load."

"Sure, but you didn't ask for that either, right?"

"Yeah, well, sometimes good things happen when you don't ask for them." He does that grin again and digs his foot into the wood chips of the playground. "All of that happened, and it led me here. To a park, under the moonlight, with someone interesting who doesn't have a boyfriend."

He winks.

Oof.

This could get messy.

Jo: Hey, how's the party?

Jo: Frankie?

Jo: Okay, it must be really good then.

Jo: Good morning! ♥ I require details. Photos. Give me something salacious.

Jo: Are you dead?

Frankie: Hahah, no. Sorry, I got distracted.

Jo: You are always on your phone, please.

Jo: I'm gonna need a good story to make up for this.

Phoenix: Well, now I have your number.

Frankie: You do. That much is fairly evident.

Phoenix: What to do with it though?

Phoenix: Perhaps more of my awful poems?

Phoenix: Through texts or photos of poorly scrawled on pages?

Frankie: You could also just send me a photo of your abs.

Frankie: You know, like a normal kid in high school.

Phoenix: That. Is not my style.

Frankie: Sigh. Fine.

Frankie: A six stanza poem instead of a six pack.

Frankie: I can do that.

Phoenix: So can I.

Chapter Seven

"Joanne!" my mom snaps as we walk down the stairs. "Come on now."

Like I'm in some huge rush to hang out in a church basement. I tug at the dress I'm wearing, some wool or tweed thing that looks like it belongs in a period-piece movie, or maybe used for a professor's jacket with elbow patches. The soft mutterings of polite goodbyes and small talk from St. Genevieve's fades, making room for the loud bustle of the meeting space underneath.

The linoleum tile floor welcomes me as much as the lime-green and off-white square panels can, and my mother bursts through the already-open doors with a spring of extra energy. Her hands are immediately swept up in someone else's and hugs are exchanged, and I cower along a few feet behind her, flashing pained smiles at strangers as she introduces me around.

I've met plenty of them before. They all nod politely. An older man here, some young wife there. A few other awkward teenagers who flash me quick "it'll all be over soon" looks before returning to staring at their shoes. None of these kids go to my school, and most of these people live in this neighborhood, not in ours, which is several towns away. Maybe I wouldn't mind coming to church and these little get-togethers if I saw familiar faces that I cared about, but nope. This is the church Mom grew up in, and apparently, I have to too. I even had to do catechism school here, when all my other friends were at the church right in town.

I glance over to one of the walls where fold-out tables with pocked beige plastic surfaces are loaded up with donated pastries, coffee, and ancient tea bags. At least there's something there to distract me from all this. Little kids are running around the place, ducking under tables and chairs, collecting little multicolored plastic disks—bingo tokens, something I did when I was little too. When things were simpler, before I realized what messages this place, and therefore my mother, was trying to send me.

I make my way over to the line for snacks, snagging a flimsy paper plate with the consistency of a napkin. With all the money my parents donate here, and what I assume everyone else does, they could at least spring for some better fixings.

I fold the paper plate like a slice of pizza and fill the middle up with doughnut holes. They aren't exactly soft, more golf ball–like. Then I scour the seats on the other side of the room. It looks like about a good quarter of the church is in here from earlier, a mixture of adults milling about near the door and the coffee, the rest sitting on fold-out metal chairs at rickety tables—maybe lunch tables? I know there's a junior high Catholic school at Holy Spirit, the church that's actually in my neighborhood where a few of my friends go, and I wonder if St. Genevieve's school hosts breakfasts or lunches down here.

"Joanne!" my mom shouts, and I wince. No matter how often I tell her to call me "Jo," she still leads with that. She waves me over to a table, some unfamiliar faces sitting around her. I walk over, trying not to scratch at this stupid dress as it nips at my thighs and calves. This is all such bullshit. I feel like I'm cosplaying at the worst comic con of all time with the shittiest costume.

This isn't who I am, and what makes it all worse is that she knows it. And so do her friends.

"You remember the Forsters, right?" she asks, gesturing at the couple sitting across from her. Next to the dad there's a teen boy staring into his lap, looking just as miserable as I feel. He glances up at me, a soft smile escaping his face. He looks just old enough to be ready to graduate this Catholic school, maybe thirteen, with dark brown hair and freckles that match.

"Yeah, sure," I say, even though I don't. I hold a hand out to the kid. "Jo."

"Joanne," Mom interjects, "correcting" me.

I turn back toward my mom and glare at her, and she just smirks.

"Gareth," the kid squeaks out, taking my hand lightly.

He goes back to staring down, and I manage to get a peek at a book in his lap, though I can't make out what it is.

"Nice to see you again," Mrs. Forster says as I sit down next to my mom. "It's been a while, hasn't it? I feel like I don't see you at the after-church gatherings anymore." This question isn't so much for me as it is for my mom, and the woman looks right at her. It's certainly *about* me, though.

"It has." Mom nods. "School's been a bit busy, though, and someone's got her clubs."

"Mom," I grumble.

"What kind of clubs?" Mrs. Forster coos, leaning on the table.

"Oh, these social justice warrior—"

"Social justice club." It's my turn to interject, and I glare back at Mom when she turns to scowl at me. "We call it SMAAC, for Social Movements and Advocacy Club. We try to make our peers at school take a closer look at injustices happening not just at school but outside the walls."

"Hm." Mrs. Forster nods. "I was thinking maybe . . . you were in bands or something."

"What causes do you fight for?" Mr. Forster chimes in, his head tilted a little. He looks genuinely curious and interested, which gets him a glare from both his wife and my mom. "What?" he asks in response to their stares, and the two of them just suck at their teeth.

He kinda reminds me of Dad.

"Well, last week we had a rally regarding free tampons in the bathrooms at school. Apparently, there was a motion to actually do this, but it got struck down by the school board." I try my hardest not to look over at Mom, and I can almost feel the frustration radiating off her.

She's *on* the school board.

"Oh." Mr. Forster nods. "That sounds reasonable, though—"

"Larry," Mrs. Forster snaps.

"What?" he scoffs back. "Don't a lot of schools in the region give out free condoms—"

"Larry!" she almost shouts.

"Jesus Christ, Barbara. 'Condoms' isn't a curse word," Mr. Forster groans, and everything about his expression tells me he's been dealing with this for a while. Gareth is looking up from his book a little as his dad talks, his eyes cautiously exploring what's unraveling at the table. "They give them away for free in the nurse's office at Gareth's school, so why not . . ." He stumbles a little and looks at me. "It's not 'feminine hygiene products' anymore, right? That's not an inclusive way to talk about them?"

This cracks a smile out of me.

"I'm trying," he says. I glance back over at Mom and Mrs. Forster, who look like they are about to explode, and Gareth is staring down at his book, grinning. "It's nice that you're following a passion where you're helping other people."

"Thanks," I say. I think that's the first time someone has ever said something positive about me in this place. Or at least, something genuinely positive that wasn't about making me more like someone else. Always it's, *You have so much potential, if only you could . . .* and other such statements. I feel a little seen right now.

"All right, well," Mrs. Forster grumbles, fussing with her coat and pulling a purse up from off the floor. "I think we should probably get going."

"Oh, come on, Barb—"

"No," she snaps back.

"You need to learn to try harder for—" Mr. Forster stops, his mouth a thin line. He shakes his head, gritting his teeth, and I can't help but notice Gareth shrinking a little more in his seat.

Oh.

"Not *here*," Mrs. Forster says, her tone stern and final. "I'll give you a call, Stacy. We'll get coffee."

"I'd like that," Mom says, smiling. But when she turns back to me, her expression sours.

"Fine," Mr. Forster agrees, seeming to give in. "Come on, Gareth."

Gareth looks up at his dad and then over at me, sighs a little, and pushes out from the table, that book tucked away under his arm. The family walks toward the exit and staircase, and for a second, I catch Gareth turning around, looking over toward me.

And damn if I don't see something of myself there, all those years ago.

Dad and Mom, fighting in this space. One fighting for me. The other not.

And now I'm stuck with the "winner" of that fight. Dad stays home, stays out of these conversations. Worn down by Mom, like a thumbtack that's been pressed into a cork-board. And I'm not sure if I'll ever be able to forgive him for letting himself be silenced. He's supposed to want to go to battle for me, the way Mr. Forster just did. I only hope for Gareth that he doesn't lose that fire.

Or let someone else put it out.

"Joanne, you can't just talk like that here." My mom sighs, rubbing her forehead with her hands. "We have an image to maintain, a standard, and if you can't just—"

"Oh, fuck this." I stand up, kicking the folding chair out from under me. It clatters to the hard floor with an awful metallic bang.

"Hey!" Mom shouts, but I'm already weaving around the chairs and tables and people, strangers staring at me as I hustle away. "Joanne, you get back here . . ."

Her voice fades, echoing in the stone stairwell that leads out of the basement and back into the church. The dark staircase leading away from the lime-green floor-ing and shitty furniture to the warm shades of mahog-any pews and the shimmering stained glass of the actual church is always a jolt. The place is mostly cleared out now, a few stragglers still in their pews, some clergy members still up by the front, talking to people.

And Gareth, walking along the side aisle toward the exit. His parents are walking down the center aisle of the church, visibly arguing. Their words are whispered, but their intention isn't, as they keep gesturing with their hands, their faces turned up in fury. Why not just let it all out? Who is gonna care? None of these people matter.

"Hey." I catch up to Gareth and lightly touch his shoulder. He turns around, that book clutched in his hands. There are two teen boys in silhouette on the cover, and he holds it close to his chest like it's something precious. I know that author's books, and I know what he's doing: diving into some pages in order to feel seen. I get it.

"What?" he asks, his eyes searching around, looking anywhere but at mine. They settle on his parents, fighting in the middle of the church, and he shakes his head, staring down.

"Nothing, just . . ." I look behind me, for my mom, for his parents, for anyone. "I just want you to know that I see you. And other people will too. This . . ." I gesture around. "It's not forever."

He smiles a little and, with a quick sniff, nods and continues walking out of the church.

I watch him leave, turning into one of the silhouettes on that book as the bright sunlight shines against him when walking out the doors.

It's like a time machine, watching this happen. That was me there, once upon a time, and in some ways, it still is.

And I just hope I didn't lie to him.

"Joanne!" My mom's voice echoes through the empty church like a thunderclap, and I turn around. She's standing by the stairwell entry, crossed arms holding both our jackets. She storms toward me, and I can feel the last few remaining eyes in the church staring at us. "Do you just need attention?" she snaps. "Is that what this is all about?"

"I actually would like less, Mom. You won't leave me alone."

"You're just going to make your life harder!"

"Trust me . . . it's hard enough as is."

"You're going to come back downstairs with me, and we're going to have a talk with Father Colt."

"Mom, come on—"

"No, we're going to have a chat about . . ." She's looking right at me and just waves her hand around. "All this. Let's go."

She turns on her heel like someone in the military, and I follow.

She doesn't have to say it.

All this just means me.

• • •

When I was little, there were these routines after church. Mom, Dad, and I, and sometimes a random family they'd become pals with at a recent event, gathered up in a restaurant. More often than not it was a local diner not too far from the church, where I'd order the same platter of chicken fingers and curly fries every single time, but sometimes we'd head to a chain restaurant—a TGI Fridays or a Ruby Tuesday—where once again, I'd find chicken fingers.

But the more I changed, the more these routines shifted. Though I still want chicken fingers no matter where I go.

When I started asking questions about church and about religion, the diner with new families and church friends became a thing of the past. It was the chain restaurants all the time and just us. A booth in the back. Or sometimes a drive-through run at whatever fast food was on the way home. The faster, the better. When I began dressing in ways that made me feel more myself and started fighting against Mom's image of me, we went to later sermons—in the afternoon, with the church half empty.

These days, she mercifully drops me off at Amy's after church, a café that's not too far from home. Frankie always meets me there, to decompress, to bullshit, to just be us. I'm not sure why I still go with Mom to church in the first place, really. I know I could probably get away with staying home by making an entire scene. But as furious as she makes me and as much as I hate all of it, I'm hoping that maybe, just maybe, she'll figure out that it's not me who changed.

It's just the routine that did. The way she's used to things.

I've always been this way. It's who I am.

I step out of the car onto the mostly empty Sunday afternoon sidewalk. I close the door and peer inside the passenger window. Mom is staring ahead, hands gripping the steering wheel, eyes focused on something I can't quite see. And that's the problem, I think.

"Mom, look, I'll—"

"Just be home by dinner," she says, shaking her head a little. The car juts forward and I stagger back, watching as she disappears down the street, past all the boutiques and tiny eateries that dot the small downtown strip. All places she won't go with me. There used to be weekend trips to the ice-cream joint and after-school runs to the bakery to get the last batches of doughnuts or cupcakes before it closed—dollar desserts that were a tiny bit stale but still tasted sweet.

I scratch at the ugly dress and turn to duck into Amy's. It's a small place with a quirky, vintage feel on the inside. Large plush couches and enormous pillows on the floor, where students at the local college just sprawl out like cats. The owner, Amy, used to be a dancer once upon a time, and this café was her studio. You can make out the large floor-to-ceiling mirrors along the walls, hidden behind bookcases and vintage picture frames. The cracks between shelves and tables make it look like there's maybe a hidden, bigger world beyond them. Retiring to a life of coffee, tea, and whatever music you want on the café stereo sounds spectacular to me.

Frankie sits at a table alone, fussing with her phone. She's got on another messy sweater, so old that I can see the pearls of fabric and string bunched up on the surface and shoulders. I walk over, smiling. I love picking those little balls of lint off her sweaters, and I think she knows it, saving them just for me. Her eyes flit up and she puts her phone down on the table quickly.

"Oh?" I grin, nodding at the little brick on the table, the surface patterned in an artificial stonework print. "Texting your other girlfriend?"

"What? No." Frankie snorts, sputtering a laugh. She's

so cute when she's flustered, my God. I press my hands down against the table in front of her and lean over, kissing her on the forehead, her hair smelling richly of vanilla. I just want to disappear into her arms right now, in the quiet warmth of this café.

I pull a chair over and sit down.

"So how was the party?" I ask, inching closer. "It sounded like a blast from everyone on social media. Kelsey texted me, said you bailed early. You know I need you there to give me all the details."

"Sorry." She laughs a little and grabs her phone. "It was just the typical teenage ratfuck."

"Well, probably better than what I just dealt with. Another church social hour after the sermon, and I get thrown to the wolves for talking back to some homophobic mom," I grumble, leaning back. "Do you know that God will forgive your 'gay feelings' as long as you don't act on them? Thanks, Father Colt." I snort out a laugh. "Father Colt. He sounds like a high school football player who couldn't make it and decided to try to make touchdowns for the Lord." I cross my arms, and Frankie is still staring at her phone. "Hey, you there?"

"Yeah, sorry," she says, putting her phone back down.

"Was that guy there?" I ask.

"Guy?"

"Come on, that new kid. What's his name?" I squint, trying to remember. "He's clearly super into you. I saw him doting on you in the hallway on Friday."

"Oh!" she exclaims. "You saw that?"

"It was cute," I say. "What, did he read you a letter or something? Poor guy."

"Yeah." She laughs a little. "Yeah, he was there. I don't know, I left early."

"Well, let's see what happened, load up the social media highlight reel." I get up and sit next to her on the big plush bench, our backs against the wall. I nuzzle up closer to her, and she leans against me. I feel my whole body sigh, with her close like this. Like everything that just happened at the after-church bullshit is leaving as I sit here being my true self—save for the clothes.

Frankie pulls back up and reaches out, scratching the fabric of the dress with a finger. Her mouth turns down in a scowl.

"Yeah, it's not exactly snuggling friendly." I laugh a little. "I really should try to sneak a change of clothes sometime. Or you could bring them!" I rub my hands together, scheming a little, and she grins. I'm over at the Healys' house enough that it wouldn't be terribly suspect for me to just leave a few outfits over. "But on to more important things."

I pull my phone out and swipe over to Instagram, and I glance at Frankie doing the same. My feed is full of the usual this morning: some ads, some artfully taken photos of coffee, a few celebrities and photos of their wildly beautiful homes. A handful of my favorite authors complaining about writing, and they all remind me of Frankie, who seems to love it so much while also hating it.

But I suppose that's the thing about fighting to have a voice. It's work, even when using it brings you joy.

And then something flashes across my screen, and I stop scrolling and drop my phone onto the table, not sure what I just saw.

Did I . . .

I pick it back up and drop it again, the image hitting me like a jolt of electricity. Like I just touched my tongue to a nine-volt battery.

"What is it?" Frankie asks, reaching for my phone.

"Don't," I say, grasping her hand. "I . . . It's bad." I swallow.

"Jo," Frankie presses, looking up at me, her face awash in worry. "What's going on?"

I let go of her hand and slide my phone over. She turns it around, her eyes on the screen, silent. She takes a sharp breath and puts it down . . . and then turns it back around, taking a screenshot. I hear the camera sound of it without looking down, and it jolts me again.

"What are you doing?!" I snap, pulling the phone away. "You can't—"

"Someone is going to delete that," she says grimly. "And it'll be like it never happened. Proof is important."

I clear my throat. "Proof?"

"That was Bella," Frankie says, and her face is full of fury. "And I recognize that room. That's Andrew's house, that's Andrew's *bedroom*."

"I-I know it's Bella, but . . ." I stammer out. "Shit."

Frankie takes my phone again and flips back to Instagram. I can barely look at the photo. It's Bella Fox, looking very passed out on a bed, her shirt pulled up to her shoulders. Her phone is beside her, the sheets all rumpled around her. Was she reaching for her phone when she fell asleep? When she . . .

"People are such assholes." I feel like I'm about to cry and wipe at the corners of my eyes.

"Nothing about this is okay," Frankie says, shifting about in her seat. She grabs her tattered backpack full of enamel pins and hefts it up onto the table, before pulling her phone out again.

"What are you doing?" I ask.

"Writing down the handles of everyone who commented on the photo," she says, angrily scratching odd screen names with strings of numbers onto her notepad. The original account looks like some sort of burner name. I don't recognize it, but the people who shared it . . . those accounts I know. We tap through their respective stories—some of them drew pictures on top of her. These are not friends of mine by any means, but people I've seen in classes and in the halls.

"We're going to need to call these people out," Frankie continues, taking screenshots of her own. "And we need to go check on Bella." She gets up and reaches for her coat. "Let's go see if she's okay, let her know we have her back, that she's supported."

"Wait, what?" I ask. "Right now?" I edge out of the seat.

"Remember our mission statement that we wrote for SMAAC? Protect the voiceless, be proactive about reaching out?"

"Frankie, come on." I sigh. "We're the only ones in the club."

"That's because we're the only ones who care," she presses. "This isn't just some high school drama or party gossip, the kind that we can sit around and laugh at and enjoy. This is wrong. Something terrible happened, and to someone we know."

Frankie moves around the table and spins to look at me. I haven't moved, but I feel like I can't.

"What is it?" she asks.

"You're just . . . so amazing. I love how much you care about other people. I love . . . goddamn. I love you."

She smiles in a way that looks like she might cry.

"I love you too." She steps forward and grabs my hands in hers. "Now, let's go show Bella how much we love her."

Frankie: Hey, where are you right now?

Frankie: Are you seeing all this stuff on Instagram?

Frankie: Do you know anything about it?

Frankie: Nick?

Chapter Eight

Nick

The chain basketball net sings as Andrew sinks another free throw, and I groan, looking up at the morning sky. My head is throbbing impossibly hard, my stomach keeps churning, and I'm starting to think our usual routine of jogging the neighborhood and shooting hoops on Sunday was . . . a poor decision today. Perhaps, just perhaps, I should have taken this morning off.

"Boom!" Andrew smiles, his teeth bright white, his blond hair shining in the sun. It's as though powering through endless shots and bottles of craft beer has zero effect on him and his body. "You're up."

He bounces the ball on the black asphalt, and I nearly miss it. I fumble to grab it as a bit of bile rises up the back of my throat. I wince and swallow it back. Ugh.

"Well, well." He grins, hands on his hips. "I can't believe I'm witnessing your first hangover. Feels like a real friendship milestone. We're bonded, bro."

"Shut up." I groan and walk over to him. I shoot and

the ball bricks loudly off the metal rim and bounces off into some nearby overgrown grass. The parks department doesn't exactly maintain things in the winter, and it doesn't take into account teen jocks going on runs and playing H-O-R-S-E on Sunday mornings.

"You should be proud," he says as I fetch the ball. "You only threw up twice on our jog."

"I hate you," I grumble, walking back with the ball.

"It was such an *insane* night," Andrew says. I throw the ball angrily at him, hard, and he catches it, the rubber making a *knnng!* sound in his palms. "I'm glad you were there. I hope there's . . . you know, no hard feelings."

I glare at him.

I was hoping we wouldn't even talk about this. I can barely remember most of the evening anyway, but one part is clear:

Him disappearing with Bella.

"It's fine," I say, forcing the words out.

"I mean, Bella was just all over me. What was I supposed to do?" he says, a smug little smirk on his face.

"You seemed pretty all over her too." I cross my arms. I watched the two of them all evening. Any time I thought I was going to get a second, just a second, to talk to Bella, there was Andrew, swooping in like a damn vulture. His arm around her, drinks in his hand, getting her whatever she wanted.

"I guess." He shrugs. "Such a wild night."

He shoots, the ball sinking right through the net.

"Better make that one in, or you're out." He grins.

"Right." I chase after the ball as it once again finds its way into the grass. "You know . . ." I pause, picking up the ball. "I'm just a little beside myself here. You know how I feel about her, how she feels about me—"

"Well, I mean, does she?" He smirks.

A flash of heat hits me in the chest as he just looks at me, that smug little smile still on his face, and I throw the ball out of the basketball court. It sails over the fence and into the street outside the park.

"Fuck you, Andrew," I growl, and grab my jacket off the nearby rusted-over bleachers. I can picture the two of them still, making their way up the stairs. How he high-fived someone on the way up, and how Lily bolted out of the house into the night. He was just on an emotional rampage, hurting everyone close to him . . .

Why am I even here with him?

"Come on, man!" he pleads, walking toward me. "I was just messing with you. Bros before h—"

"Don't say that. Don't you fucking say that about her," I snap, stomping toward him. He shirks back, his hands up in the air. I exhale, anger flowing through me, and I can see my breath in the sharp winter air.

"Chill, man," he says, lowering his hands. "It didn't even mean anything."

I walk away from him, hurrying toward the exit to the court.

"Nick!" he shouts after me. "Nick, come on, man!"

I don't ever want to see his face again.

Kim: Hey Bella, I know we don't talk all that much, but I saw the photo . . . Are you okay? Where are you right now? Is there anything I can do?

Bella: It's fine.

Kelsey: Hey, are you okay?

Kelsey: Need anyone?

Bella: I'm okay.

Andrew: Hey can we talk about last night?

Andrew: It was so crazy, I know things got a little out of hand, but I had fun.

Andrew: Did you have fun? It seemed like you had fun.

Andrew: Bella?

Hannah: Just checking in on you.

Bella: I'm good.

Chris: Bella what the hell. Are you okay?

Chris: Who took that photo?

Chris: I'm going to kill them.

Bella: Don't tell Mom. Please. Please don't tell Mom.

Emily: Hey, what are you doing right now?

Emily: Let's go get coffee. Let's get you out of the house.

Bella: Thanks. I'm good right now.

Chapter Nine

Bella

Shit.

I lost count after the tenth text this morning, so I'm not even sure what this one is. But my notifications on social media are still a complete, lit-up disaster, from people direct messaging me to the . . . photo. Me. Passed out on Andrew's bed. My T-shirt up. Just sprawled out for the entirety of our high school and God knows who else to see, like a knocked-over department store mannequin, there to be played with by anyone strolling by.

All the messages on social media are the same—"I don't know if you've seen this but . . ."—while my texts are full of invites to go out, get support, and the like. Most are from people I haven't really spoken to in forever or just studied with once or twice. My cousin Chris somehow saw it, which sends me reeling. I just need this to pass over before Mom or Dad see it.

Ugh. Andrew. I was there to talk to Nick. How could I have . . .

There's a jab in my skull. This headache is unbelievable. I like going hard at parties. I do. I cut loose, I dance, but . . . I always remember everything. All the little details, the laughter and the joy and the drama. That's the point of it all, right? Making memories, being light and full of life. But this feels different. Something is different. Like someone took the night away from me in their fist.

And the texts and direct messages won't stop coming. Like everyone has to make sure I've seen this. Like they're the first ones to break the news.

Courtney: Hey, are you okay? I saw the photo circulating. We'll find out who made that account and beat their ass.

Aileen: Just wanted to check in on you. I saw the picture.

Jeff: Hey, have you seen this? Are you all right?

Lily: You bitch. That's my boyfriend. I thought we were friends.

I wince at Lily's message. I'm . . . not sure why I would do this to her. I don't know her terribly well; we've hung out a few times at lunch and on trips, but that's really it. Ugh, but I knew how much Andrew was smitten with me. I try to shake her hurt out of my head, and there's that throbbing still. I wouldn't do that to her. To anyone, really. I wouldn't do anything with Andrew for that matter. I'm not into him, it's not like that.

I've been hungover before. Plenty. But nothing like this. Nothing at all like this.

I fire off another series of texts to Nick.

Me: Hey.

Me: Sorry we didn't get a chance to hang out last night.

Me: I know we were supposed to like talk.

Me: Nick?

He's not answering, and it's leaving this hollow feeling in my chest. I screwed that up by doing . . . whatever I did with Andrew. Ugh.

I take a breath and exhale. Monday. Okay. Tomorrow's going to be awful. School. Everyone's judging eyes. For every single person messaging me, there's probably a good dozen or so people I don't know who have seen this. That's how it works, right? But it'll fade. Everyone will forget by the end of the week, and we'll be on to the next slice of drama. That's this town, I know it. You keep your head down, and people move on.

I just have to pray Mom and Dad don't see this. That one of my idiot classmates doesn't show it to their parents.

Whew. Anxiety swells in my chest. I'm going to be carrying this fear for a while.

It's okay. People will forget. It'll all go away—

"Bella?"

I jump in my bed, and my bedroom door creaks open. Mom peeks in, her eyes searching me, a little smile on her face. My heart is absolutely pounding in my chest. This is it. She's seen the photo, she's read the social media updates, someone, somewhere, told her—

"You awake?" she asks, stepping into the room delicately. The two of us look wildly alike, which makes for annoying boys telling me how hot my mom is. God, if I had a dollar for every stupid comment from Andrew about wanting to "bang" my mother—

Andrew.

"Hey," I mutter, sitting up in my bed.

"Getting a bit late," she says, smiling a little at me. "Someone maybe had a bit too much fun at that party?"

"Mom," I groan. But I'm relieved. This conversation doesn't seem to be heading the way I feared. She doesn't know. She hasn't seen.

"It's fine. You know I don't really care as long as you're being safe and getting home." She hands me a tumbler I didn't notice was in her hand. I pop it open, and the smell of coffee wafts over me like a warm blanket.

"You're just the best." And she is. Supportive and altogether there, she's a rock in the face of so much. It almost makes me want to tell her, but the idea that she might crumble makes me rethink all of it. This could be the thing that breaks her.

"Oh, shush." She waves me off, heading back out of my room. "But get yourself together. Two of your friends are here downstairs."

"What?" I ask. "Way to bury the lede there, Mom." I force myself up, my whole body fighting with me. It's almost like I'm still drunk, but mentally I feel very here. It makes no sense.

It's not the first time I've come home from a party having had a few too many. Mom never really cares. I mean, she does. She wants me to be safe, and I always am. No driving. Have a friend who has your back. Try not to come home too late. Don't party with strangers. She lays out rules, and I do my best to follow them. She's been a great buffer with Dad, who would probably be slightly pissed.

Not sure who had my back last night, though. It's all a bit of a blur, and I'm not even sure how I got home. Did I walk from Andrew's? That feels impossible; my house is on the other side of the big park, and there's no way I'd stroll through there that late at night.

I throw on my pants from last night and a new shirt and make my way downstairs, taking each step carefully, still feeling all kinds of woozy. The one upside to all of this? At least Mom didn't come barging into my room shouting about how *not* careful I was, seeing as there's a nearly shirtless photo of me circulating around my entire high school less than twenty-four hours later.

And there, in my living room, sit Frankie Healy and

Jo Taylor, sipping on coffee on our couch. I remember Frankie bailing the party early with that hot new kid, who looks like a Jonas brother blended with a vintage thrift shop. And the way their eyes flit up to me, both of them, cups in their hands, tells me everything.

They've seen it.

"Hey," Frankie starts, getting up.

Not here, I mouth silently, before talking. "Hey, you." I smile. "What's up, Jo?"

"Hey?" Jo says, her tone the same as Frankie's.

Is this what it's going to be like? The quiet pity in the voices of my friends and the laughter from those who aren't? I mean, I haven't heard anyone laughing yet. My notifications haven't been negative, save for Lily's; it's mostly been people messaging me to make sure I'm aware of what happened. But it's only a matter of time. I know it.

I nod toward the door.

"Mom, we'll be right back!" I shout toward the kitchen.

"Okay!" she says, and I hear some dishes clattering about. "Wear a jacket!"

The girls and I make our way out the front door, and I stop after I shut it, leaning against it on our little patio. I cross my arms.

"Well?" I ask. "I've seen it. I know."

"Yeah, I mean, we figured," Frankie says, looking down at her shoes for a moment.

"We wanted to make sure, you know?" Jo says, her face turned up in a wince.

"Yeah, you and, like, two dozen other people at school, all messaging and texting me," I scoff.

"Ugh, I'm sorry. If you want to talk about it . . ." Frankie takes a step forward. "I just want you to know that we're there for you."

"Frankie, I . . ." I exhale. "I like you and Jo, I mean, obviously, but . . . why would I want to talk about it with you guys? Or anyone, really?"

"That's fair." Jo nods and looks over at Frankie, a beat of awkward silence between all of us. I feel like Jo wants to bail, something I appreciate. She catches the implied social cue of "I'm fine, please leave," but Frankie doesn't.

"It's just . . . sometimes it can be hard to know who is there for you in moments like this. And it's not okay that someone did that to you without your consent."

I squint at her, and my throat goes suddenly dry. I clear it. "Did . . . did someone say something to you about what happened?" I ask, trying to recall more of last night. The drinks, the dancing, Andrew . . . It's all still a blur. "Did Nick say something?"

"Nick?" Frankie asks, glancing at Jo.

"I mean, I remember . . . I was doing shots with him and Andrew." A little bit of the night comes back, like snapshots scattered across my mind. "And then . . ." I shake my head. "I don't know, I remember throwing up in a trash can by the bed, and then Andrew and me doing . . . something?

"But it was like . . ." I swallow. "You ever fall asleep,

wake up, but you can't quite open your eyes? You're there, but it's like you're frozen, and it takes a minute to shake out of it? It was like that, like I was just stuck there. And the next thing I know, it's morning, I'm here." I glance at my house. "I'm not even sure how I got home."

Frankie and Jo are looking at each other, their faces aghast.

"What?" I ask.

"Bella . . . that's . . ." Frankie shakes her head. "If Andrew did something to you . . . that's rape. You know that, right?"

"No," I scoff, my heart suddenly racing. "No, no way. It was just . . . I was a little out of it, that's all. Andrew wouldn't . . . he couldn't. No."

"Look, do you want to . . ." Frankie nods at the door. "Do you want to tell your mom? Do you want us here with you when you tell—"

"No, no," I spit out. "She's the last person I want to tell. I was hoping the stupid photo would just blow over and she'd never know. Do you have any idea what something like this would do to her? She's like a . . . a mother from a sitcom. She's not ready to have a very special episode. And my dad?! He's the same, which means he'll probably go try to beat up Andrew's dad or something."

"Do you know who took the photo?" Jo asks. Frankie looks at her. "I mean, if Andrew and Nick were there . . ."

"You don't think Nick would have *let* that happen?!" Frankie gasps. "No. I . . . did he?"

Frankie's looking at me.

Jo is looking at me.

It suddenly feels like everyone is looking at me, not just these two, and something just seizes up in my chest.

"I . . . I don't know!" I almost shout, and I can see my hands are trembling.

"Maybe we should go to the police," Jo says.

"Are you fucking kidding me?!" I snap, and turn back to the door. "Like I'm really going to walk over there and say Andrew Montefiore . . ." I lower my voice now. "Everyone, *everyone*, in this town worships his family. There's a statue of his great-grandfather in the downtown plaza near that coffee shop you two hang out at all the time."

They look at each other, surprised.

"What?" I sniff. "I go there too. You two aren't exactly secret agents. No one is going to believe me. When something like this happens, no one believes anybody anyway. Who is going to believe me?"

"*We* believe you," Jo says, taking a step toward me.

"Why do you two even care about what happened?" I ask, turning away. "We aren't that close."

"Hey," Frankie presses, and I glance back at her. She swallows. "Because it could happen to any of us."

Frankie: Nick, you need to pick up your phone.

Frankie: Or answer a text, anything!

Frankie: Do you have any idea what happened?! Is that why you're hiding?

Frankie: Nick ANSWER ME.

Chapter Ten

Nick

I walk into my house and toss my sweaty track jacket onto a hook on the wall, then promptly take it off. It'll be a whole thing with Mom if she spots it there, still wet and cold, though she's nowhere to be found. Both she and Dad just weren't here this morning, a little note on the fridge telling me and Frankie to "order in, we'll be back later."

I want to hope the two of them are on, like, a date or something, which I'm aware is a little weird. Hoping your parents are out somewhere, holding hands, eating something too expensive. But I want them to be *normal*, especially with me leaving soon. Frankie deserves that much. I make my way upstairs and throw my coat into my room and close the door just as the front door to the house swings open again. All the opening and shutting rattles my hungover brain, and I head back down, wincing at the creaking of the stairs.

"Nick? Nick!"

Frankie is shouting, and I can hear her stomping

around the house before I see her. I hop off the stair, landing and peering in the living room.

"There you are. Did you get my texts?"

"Texts?" I ask. I pull my phone out, and it's absolutely lit up with notifications. "Oh, damn, sorry, no. I was out running and playing basketball. What's up?"

"What's up?!" she snaps. "Are you kidding me?!"

"What . . ." I groan and run my hand through my hair. "Can you keep it down? I'm crazy hungover from Andrew's, and he put me through it this morning."

"You *saw* him?!" She sounds horrified.

"Yeah, we work out every Sunday . . . Is something wrong?"

"Yeah," she says, crossing her arms. "Andrew. That's exactly it. Don't you have anything to say about him? You guys had your morning run and your bro time, so what did you talk about?"

"What are you going on about?!" I yell. She looks like she's about to boil over, the way she does when she and Mom are fighting, but here I am, having done nothing.

"You mean to tell me you *didn't* see what happened," she says, her tone flat. She storms toward me with her phone out and flips to something before handing it to me.

Bella's on the screen.

Her shirt is up.

She's on Andrew's bed.

She does . . . not look aware of what's happening.

Or happened.

Oh no.

"I'm going to kill him." I grit my teeth, balling my fists. I glance back up at Frankie, her face full of worry. I exhale, loosening my hands, and I can feel my nails plucking out of my palms. I can't believe he would . . . He said he was going to take care of her.

"You shouldn't get involved in this." I shake my head. "We . . . I don't know if we should. But you definitely shouldn't. I'll go handle Andrew."

"What?!" Frankie yells, pulling the phone back. "Showing up and kicking Andrew's ass doesn't fix anything. Did you not just see this?! Don't you care about her? She wasn't able to say yes. She wasn't able to have a say. You were supposed to look out for her. You're supposed to—"

"I can't look out for *everybody*, Frankie!" I shout. She cowers, and I breathe out. "I'm sorry, but I can't. I can't look out for you, for Mom, for Bella, for Dad, for every single person in my life at the same time. I'm sick of it. I'm sick of all of it."

"What's going on here?" someone who isn't me or Frankie asks.

It feels like all the air has just been ripped out of the room.

Mom is standing by the front door, her car keys still in her hand. Her eyes are a little bloodshot, like she maybe didn't sleep at all last night. My heart is racing madly in my chest, and that blending with my pounding headache makes me feel like I'm going to throw up again. I've tried so hard to be good, to be perfect, to watch out for everyone and just keep my head down, and now it's all going to completely unravel.

"Don't say *anything*," I whisper to Frankie.

Frankie launches into it anyway. "Mom, you know Bella—"

"She *thinks* Andrew assaulted her at the party," I interrupt, and immediately hate myself.

"Thinks?" Frankie snaps.

"What do you mean assaulted?" Mom asks, her brow furrowed. She walks toward us, but she's moving weirdly slow. I look over at Frankie, but she doesn't seem to notice it, she's just glaring at me like she can burn holes through my face with her eyes. "And Andrew Montefiore? That Andrew?"

"*That* one," Frankie says, venom in her voice. "Bella was raped. Andrew forced himself on her when she was too drunk, or too drugged, to do anything about it. And Nick was there hanging out with him at the party! He *saw* how drunk she was." She whips back to me, lashing out. "You were there. You need to come with us to the police!"

I look back at her, and the rage has been replaced with a look of pleading. I wince, my headache pounding, trying to recall more of the night: Andrew flirting with Bella all night, following her around, popping up whenever we had a moment to ourselves to talk . . .

Like he was trying to herd her around the house, away from me. From anyone.

He said he'd take care of her when she was too many drinks in and . . .

132

No. He couldn't.

He *wouldn't*.

"Nick . . ." Frankie presses, looking at me intently. "Come on, I . . . Don't make me go there, of all places, to see a bunch of cops without you." She looks at Mom and grimaces. Mom won't get it. But I do.

"Frankie—" I start.

"You can't just go calling the police because some girl got drunk and there's a bunch of he said, she said. You'll end up ruining that poor boy's life," Mom chimes back in. "If someone drinks herself to the point where she doesn't know what's going on, these things happen. We're all responsible for our own actions."

There's a beat. A pause. And so much is in there and unsaid.

I feel like that's the awful victim-blaming thing you don't say out loud, and Mom just came out and said it.

And even though I'm not entirely sure what happened, bits are floating to mind, and I know that what Mom is saying is completely off base. Something isn't right. That photo. Andrew leading her around. His weird apology on the basketball court that made it seem like . . . like she was the one who wanted something to happen, without actually apologizing for a damn thing. Not to her.

"Hey, Mom, I don't know if—" I start.

"How?" Frankie interjects, her tone crushed. "How can you *say that*, Mom? How can you stand there and say something like that?"

"A girl got drunk, and someone took advantage," Mom continues, just barreling ahead with all the wrong things. I want to say something. But what good is it going to do? I just need to keep my head down, think about last night. Remember everything that happened, pull those details out. And after all this blows over, figure out a way to fix Mom and fix Frankie and fix—

Just fix all this.

"You can't go and make this your new cause of the week," Mom says, turning to walk up the stairs.

"Cause of the week?!" Frankie shouts, storming over. "Why . . . ? Why did I think you, you of all people, would understand?"

She walks right by Mom and toward the front door, but Mom keeps looking ahead and then up the stairs, her gaze somewhere else. Somewhere far away. Frankie grabs the doorknob and swings the door open and turns back to glare at me.

"I'm so fucking disappointed in you," she says, and with that, she's gone.

I glance back at Mom, who has a hand pressed up against the wall.

"Nick, were . . . you drinking?" she asks, not looking at me.

"Does that even matter?" I ask, walking toward her.

"I told you," she says, breathing heavily. "I told you this party was a bad idea. There is no reason for you to get involved in any of this. In whatever Frankie is doing, in all this . . . don't you go and—"

"Borrow trouble." I finish the sentence for her, one of her favorite little sayings.

She reaches down from the steps and pats my cheek with one hand, though it's like she's moving in slow motion still.

"Good boy," she says. "That's my good boy."

She makes her way up the stairs, quietly, slowly, and vanishes up to the second floor.

Frankie: Hey, we're on our way over, want us to pick up anything?

Jo: Yeah like water maybe? Snacks?

Bella: Are we going to the fucking movies?!

Bella: I'm fine. I don't need a bag of Skittles.

Bella: Oh God. Sorry.

Bella: I'm not terribly excited about this.

Frankie: It's okay. Your feelings are valid here.

Jo: Maybe a book? I'll pack an extra battery for our phones.

Bella: Why are you guys packing like we're going on a hike or a road trip?

Bella: It's the police station. We don't need trail mix.

Jo: Yeah, but we don't know how long it'll take for someone to talk to us.

Jo: To you.

Jo: And I don't want you sitting there getting anxious with nothing to focus on.

Bella: Ah, okay. I get it.

Bella: Thank you.

Bella: So, we have a group chat now, huh?

Bella: Hm. I sure do wish it could have been about something else. Anything else.

Frankie: Me too.

Frankie: But it still can be.

Frankie: This won't be your only story to share with us, Bella.

Chapter Eleven

Phoenix

I don't know why I'm so nervous walking into this new coffee shop. I mean, it's new to me. London Fog. It's not new to anyone else; I can tell by the way everyone in here seems to be so . . . comfortable. Like they're just a part of the soft couches and wooden chairs they are sitting on. I feel like if any of these people get up, there will be a perfect indent where they were sitting. Even on the stools that look like they're made of wrought iron.

There are warm, earth-toned furniture and Edison lights everywhere, making it feel all at once old-fashioned and modern. I see a mix of people with their laptops out, some typing away wildly, and others fiddling on their phones. I make my way over to the barista station, passing by a large bookshelf packed full of novels.

The barista must catch me staring, because he pipes up. "That's our Little Free Library."

I glance up—ALEX is on his name tag.

"We get a lot of kids in here, try to give them something else to do than . . . well . . ." He nods at a table a few feet away from us: two people on their phones, empty cups in front of them. I laugh a little, and he beams a smile. He's got a stubbly beard and round glasses that make him look like he'd be perfectly at home as a librarian as much as a café owner.

"What can I get you?"

I glance up at the chalkboard behind him, a wide array of drinks and pastries written in various colors; some look like they've been etched into the black surface forever, like just regular coffee, and others appear as if they've changed a thousand times, the dust of old writing clouding the surface, like milk in black coffee.

"You can probably guess this, but tea is our specialty," Alex says. "Particularly the namesake."

"London Fog?" I ask.

"Yup." He reaches for a cup. "Earl Grey tea, bit of lavender, steamed milk, dollop of vanilla . . . Feel like trying something new?"

My mind floats to the school. To Frankie and her friends, to the poetry class. To this different town we're trying to settle into, and I smile.

"Sure."

. . .

I manage to hole up at a lone table in the very corner of the café, the entire place sprawled out in front of me. I don't see anyone I recognize from school here, but then again,

I'm not sure I would, seeing as I just started last week. I don't think I can name more than a handful of people, save for Frankie.

Frankie.

Ever since she read that poem in class, since I walked with her down the hall, since I shared my own scribblings while pressed against a locker . . . she's been all I can think about. And that night after the party, in the park, under all those trees on the swings . . .

It sends my heart racing.

I was more than happy to move here, to help out Mom with Ruby, to navigate this complicated situation we're in. Because that's what you do when it's family. You find a way; you find the joy somewhere.

And I think I've found that joy. Maybe. It's all a bit fast.

I take a sip of the London Fog, and the sigh I let out is louder than expected.

"See?!" Alex shouts across the café, waving at me.

I like it here.

I double-check the time and open my laptop, loading up Google Meet from my writing calendar. When I click the link waiting for me, a handful of familiar faces are already there, excitably talking about something, until all their eyes focus on me.

"Phoenix!" Saundra and Nwayieze both shout, and there's Patrick, Lisa, and Mitchell, all smiling brightly. God, I've missed this bunch. Everybody looks the same, which, well, of course they do. I've barely been gone ten days.

"We were just going over one of Lisa's poems," Saundra says, and Lisa looks away from the screen, bashful, her blond hair swiping over her screen for just a moment. "Oh, stop it, it's good."

Everyone laughs.

"Are you all at Locke and Tea?" I ask, squinting at the backgrounds behind everyone. It kinda looks the same across every screen.

"Almost," Patrick says. "I'm home, they're out and about, enjoying the world. Babysitting."

"You're barely babysitting," Mitchell scoffs. "Where is your sister? You've been in front of your laptop this whole time. She could have taken the car out by now."

"She's four!" Patrick laughs.

"Still." Mitchell shrugs. "Kids these days are a lot more mature. I'll let you know if she shows up here."

"Shut up." Patrick rolls his eyes but then looks off-screen. "All right, I'll be back. I'm gonna go check on her."

Everyone laughs as he leaves the square on-screen, including me.

"How is it?" I ask. "How's the café, how's class, catch me up on everything."

And they do.

Saundra goes on and on about the new substitute English teacher and how she just doesn't get any of the books she's teaching. Not that Saundra doesn't get them. That the *teacher* doesn't, and each class feels like a battle between her and the sub. This is entirely unsurprising, as it seemed like she went to war with our usual teacher anyway, sparking debates constantly. Poor Mrs. Rich. Bless her for dealing with us.

Patrick has thrown himself into the school musical, something I've definitely known about, as he was doing that before we moved, and he regales me with the latest drama in drama. Someone else really wanted the role of the dentist in *Little Shop of Horrors* and has been making a fuss about it, even though the performance is just days away. And he's dating the lead dancer, a girl named Annie I think we all had a crush on at one point or another.

Mitchell's stepdad got him a motorcycle as an early Christmas gift, which is basically tearing his family apart at home in the most hilarious of ways. His mom doesn't want him getting that license, his stepdad feels like he's ready, his younger brother is furious because he wanted a scooter . . . the tension is thick and palpable and absolutely not a real problem, which makes it even funnier. Though having listened to so much of Frankie's actual problems at home, his rambles send my mind somewhere else. And I wonder how she's doing.

Lisa and Nwayieze have effectively taken up the positions of writers in residence at our favorite coffee shop, though none of that is official and they keep getting kicked out. But the two of them are determined to finish their poetry chapbooks, with plans to send them around in January. They want to be published before college.

"Have you seen my latest poem on Instagram?" Nwayieze asks.

"Ooh, I haven't!" I glance down at my phone and back

at the screen. She lifts her eyebrows and looks right at me, expectantly. "Oh, now?"

"Thank you." Nwayieze smirks, crossing her arms.

The crew laughs, and I open my phone, surprised to see a bundle of notifications on the home screen. I swipe over to Instagram and I've got a whole mess of private messages, and when I load them up . . .

What . . .

Who is this?

There's a girl in a bunch of Instagram Stories, shared by these new people I barely know at school and some strange, unnamed accounts without much on them, and she's got her shirt pulled up to her neck. Her eyes are closed, but . . . I recognize her.

The girl from the party, taking shots with Frankie's brother and those other kids.

Aren't they friends? I think? Maybe?

And why am I getting sent this? Why is anyone?

Something is terribly wrong here, and there's this sinking, awful feeling in my chest. Like I'm peering into someone's window and witnessing a crime, something I'm not supposed to see, but now that I have . . . there's no choice but to say something. Do something. You don't just stand witness to something like this without, I don't know, finding yourself moving.

"Phoenix?" Nwayieze asks, and I look back up to the screen.

"Hey, are you okay?" Saundra is looking back at me, her eyes full of worry. I can see her looking at the rest of the crew around whatever table they're at, all of them muttering to one another. "You look like you've seen a ghost."

"Yeah, no, I . . ." My mouth has gone dry, and I reach for the London Fog, taking a long sip, but it just makes me feel thirstier. "Look, I have to go. I'll . . . I'm sorry, something happened."

"Oh shit, is Ruby okay?!" Patrick asks, jostling around his laptop, the screen shaking.

"What's going on?" Mitchell presses.

"No, she's fine, she's . . . It's someone else . . ." I shake my head. "I'll talk to you all later, I'm sorry. I miss you."

Saundra starts to say something, but I shut the laptop.

I feel myself breathing heavily, and I look down at my phone, the stories of Bella replaced by whatever played next from the people I follow on here. A park. Some trees. Some flowers.

Like the horrible, shared image was never even there. Like it wasn't that big a deal that I just saw something I shouldn't have. That *they* just shared something they shouldn't have, whoever all these people are. Classmates, I think. But I don't really know any of them. I just followed most of these kids a few days ago, mindlessly swiping while looking up Frankie.

I exhale and move to call Frankie, but I can't quite bring myself to hit the call button. Is she going to want to hear from me right now? Has she already heard about this from a dozen different people? It's all over social media and she's a Very Online person. There's no way she isn't aware . . .

I rub my forehead and grit my teeth.
I'll just text.

Me: Hey are you alright?

Me: I'm seeing all this stuff online about that girl from the party? Your friend?

Me: I'm not really sure what to say, let me know if there's anything I can do.

Me: Though I understand if you don't want me in that space. You know?

Frankie: Hey.

Frankie: I'm okay, I'm looking into it.

Frankie: I appreciate you reaching out and letting me know you're thinking of us.

Frankie: Just like report the hell out of any account you see reposting that photo.

Me: Deal.

Me: I got you.

I wonder: Should I invite her here? Should I maybe try to go see her? I have no idea how to navigate this and be, I don't know, the best ally I can.

So I just sit here and try to read some poetry, swiping away from all the stories to Nwayieze's latest piece and focusing on the words of one of my brilliant friends. It offers up a warm distraction. But still, I can't forget what I saw or stop thinking about the new people in my life who are being affected. Bella. My God.

I'm not sure I can bring myself to write.

Frankie: We're on our way to the station.

Frankie: Let me know if you think of anything you need last minute.

Jo: Yeah, I brought the chargers.

Jo: Also a few books.

Frankie: Jo is like a walking library most days.

Jo: No lies detected there.

Frankie: Bella?

Frankie: Are you ready?

Bella: No.

Bella: No, I'm not.

Bella: But let's go. My mom is driving me. I'll see you there.

Chapter Twelve

Bella

The car ride downtown is mostly silent.

The quiet inside the car is broken only by the occasional sniffle from my mom, her hands gripping the steering wheel like she might break it off. I pray for no more red lights. The first one we stopped at, she let out an exhale for so long that I thought she might deflate like a balloon in the driver's seat.

The brakes squeak as she slows to a crawl in front of the police station, and I can hear her knuckles crack when she lets go of the wheel. She looks at me, her face weary, the whites of her eyes tinted red from all the crying. Or it could be from a burst blood vessel, with the shouting she and my father did. Not at me, but with each other and on the phone, raising hell with Andrew's family, who keep denying he did anything wrong.

"Are you sure?" she asks, reaching out to me. Her hand grips my shoulder. "I want you to stand up for what that . . . boy did to you. But this isn't going to be easy."

"I know," I say.

She leans back in her seat. "I'm sorry your father didn't come." She shakes her head. "It's not you. He's not mad at you. He's afraid of what he might do if he has to face that family. If Andrew showed up."

"It's okay, Mom." I clear my throat, my heart hammering in my chest. "It really is."

She glances back at me, and I realize she's crying again. "My girl. I'm so proud of you."

Relief washes over me. I don't know why I expected this to go so much differently. I just saw, I don't know, the two of them falling to pieces. But instead, ever since I told them what happened, they've been bastions of reason and resistance.

I practically throw myself over the center console of the car and hug my mom, who squeezes me tight, sniffling again. When I let go, she wipes at her face, a bit of makeup streaking her cheeks. She laughs, pulling her hands back at the black trails on her skin.

"All right." She glances at her phone, cheeks slick. "I'll be here when you're done. Let me know if they need me in there. Chances are they will."

"Okay." I open the car door and hop out, anxiety just rushing through me. "Love you, Mom."

I make my way toward the police station, and that's when I notice Frankie and Jo, sitting on the small wall lining the building, shrubs and flowers behind them. The two hop off at the same time and stroll toward me, pensive looks on both of their faces. The last time I was here was . . . I don't even know. When we were little, I think, and they did this whole "don't do drugs" talk with our middle school and took us on a tour of the station. It was all smiles and gentle warnings, while at the same time it felt like a "don't mess up or you'll come back here" kind of thing was being implied. Felt like forever ago, and now here I am.

Only I'm not the one who messed up.

Frankie and Jo keep reminding me of that. How this isn't my fault. How that photo floating around our school and among our friends and complete strangers wasn't my doing. And their words have gone from being this annoying little buzzing to a source of comfort. I'm feeling . . . strangely more determined. Like a reluctant fist that's getting tighter.

But it's not lost on me that the people I usually spend my time with, the ones I considered unshakable best friends, are missing in all this. All that laughter in the school halls and at lunch is just . . . silence. A few texts, but no one has really showed up for me. Nick has absolutely vanished. All my messages to him have gone unanswered, which feels particularly brutal. If anyone knows what happened last night, the real story, it would be him. But he can't seem to be bothered. After years of friendship, years of . . . well, whatever we were feeling, it's like I don't exist anymore.

"It would be . . . a lot easier not to go in there," I say, looking at the doors. It's an unassuming brick-and-concrete building, a small park across the street. That was one of the few parks in town all our mutual parents would drop us off at as little kids, to run around wildly on our own, saying it was safe because of this building across the street. Poston Park in the middle of town was "dangerous" and "in the middle of some woods," but we all found our way there anyway, to drink stolen beer and smoke cigarettes we snuck away.

I can see people milling about inside, and the park across the street is empty. Connecticut winter and all.

"People like Andrew know that," Frankie says. "They know it's not easy. And that's why they think they can get away with anything."

I swallow. "Everything's going to change once I go in there," I say, trying to steel myself.

Frankie offers up her hand.

I take it.

"Good," she says.

Nick: Hey. We need to talk.

Nick: Hey, asshole. You have your read receipts on.

Nick: I can tell you're getting these.

Nick: All right, I think I know what's going on here. I've watched enough Law & Order with my mom to know.

Nick: You're not answering because you know someone is going to check your phone later.

Nick: Is your dad the one handling your phone?

Nick: Hi Mr. Montefiore. Tell your son to come outside and square up.

Nick: Oh, look at that. Read receipts are either off now or you're just ignoring me.

Nick: Well, I don't care who sees this text.

Nick: I'm coming over.

Nick: And if you know what's good for you, you won't come outside.

Frankie: If they aren't going to give her justice right away, we have to fight for it.

Jo: Don't these things usually take a minute? Investigations and all that?

Frankie: It'll happen faster if there is public pressure and outcry.

Jo: Yeah?

Frankie: Definitely.

Frankie: I'm gonna get some supplies together, let's plan a rally.

Frankie: We'll do it right downtown, not too far from the police station, right by Andrew's family statue in the square.

Jo: Shit.

Jo: That's good.

Jo: Have you talked to Bella about it? This is her story, we don't want to make it about us.

Frankie: Oh, I have. She's in.

Jo: How . . . is she? I didn't want to message that group chat after, you know, in case she needed some time.

Frankie: I don't know if she's gonna want to speak at it, but we'll see. We can be as much of a voice for her as she needs or wants.

Jo: Alright, well I'm going to try to rally some of the people we've been trying to get on board with the club.

Frankie: They'll have to show up. They have to.

Jo: They will.

Chapter Thirteen

Frankie practically kicks the door open to Mr. Martinho's classroom, extra poster board under her arm, a tote packed full of art supplies over her shoulder. She barely even said hi to me when she showed up this morning. She's wearing her military-style jacket full of patches, same jean shorts from the other day. She settles down at the desk, spreading the poster boards out and sorting through the tote, when I clear my throat in the doorway.

"Hi?" I venture.

She looks up at me, back down at the boards, and up at me again, sucking at her teeth and shaking her head.

"I'm sorry, Jo." She walks over, gives me the quickest of hugs, and returns to her spread. "I'm just . . ." She pauses, her hands pressed against the surface of the desk, and takes a few big breaths. "It's all so much."

"Hey, hey." I walk over slowly and stand next to her. "It's okay. You don't have to carry it all yourself." I grab a marker and shift a poster board toward me. "It's a club, remember? We work together. What's the vision here?"

She looks up at the door and back down. "What's it even matter?"

"What?" I ask. "What do you—"

"No one's here," she says, looking up at me, her eyes a bit frantic. "I thought Nick would maybe show up—*finally* fucking show up and own up—but nope. Haven't even seen him at home *or* at school today, he left so wildly early. Probably to run with the rapist he didn't even want to stand up to. I practically woke up in an empty house. Who knows where Dad or MJ are.

"And Bella!" she exclaims, slapping the desk. "She *can't* be here. Physically can't. Staying home while the investigation is going on. It's so unfair. It's all so unfair."

"Have you heard anything about Andrew?" I ask.

"Nothing. You?"

"No, he's gone all dark on social media." I shake my head. "Lawyers are probably making him do that. Or his parents. Or both. Probably both."

"So it's just you and me again."

"Me and you." I smile a little.

She exhales through her nose and nods.

"Hey, is this the SMAAC meeting?"

I glance back at the door, surprised to hear another voice, and it's Lily. Of all the people to show up here, it's Lily.

She's got bags under her eyes, like she's been awake and crying for days, which I imagine she has. Andrew's her boyfriend and she was at that party. Frankie told me she was handing out drinks and shots. She tucks a strand of hair back behind her ear, long and strawberry blond, and bites at her lip, a piercing on one end of it.

"Lily," Frankie says, sounding as surprised as I feel. "I didn't . . . I mean, well, I didn't think you'd show up to something like this."

"Yeah, well"—she crosses her arms—"I didn't exactly see myself showing up for this either, but . . . I was there. I kept giving drinks to everyone. I kept . . ." She closes her eyes tight; her face looks like it's about to break like a piece of porcelain. "I should have stopped him. I could have stopped him. But when I saw him chasing Bella around, fawning over her like that . . . I don't know, all I saw was how jealous I was getting and not what was really happening."

"You didn't know." Frankie walks toward her, and Lily shirks away a little. "It's okay. I mean, I left the party. I could have stayed. There's that guilt we're all carrying."

"I just feel so complicit."

"What's important is that we can all show up for Bella *now*," Frankie presses. "She needs us now."

Lily looks back up at Frankie and nods, then peeks outside the class.

"You guys coming?" she shouts down the hall.

I look over at Frankie; her eyebrows are raised. After a beat, six other girls and one guy hurry into the room.

"I brought friends." She smiles a little.

"Amazing," Frankie says, reaching out and grabbing Lily's hands. "Amazing." She turns to the new crew, smiling brightly. "All right, welcome to SMAAC. We've got a rally to plan."

"Hey, Fabrics."

My heart nearly seizes in my chest.

I turn back toward the door.

It's Kelsey.

"Heeeey," I say, more surprised to see her than anyone else. "I didn't think you'd—"

"Well, Lily is wildly convincing," she says, nodding at Lily and the girls fluttering around Frankie, plucking out poster boards. "Besides, I felt kinda bad missing your last meetup. What can I do?"

"This is mostly Frankie's show, to be honest," I say, pointing toward the desk.

"Yeah?" she asks, walking up next to me. She bites her lip and then shakes her head. "You know, I felt like there was a good pickup line in all of that, something about wanting to see you in action . . . but I'm a little burned out today."

"Wh-what?" I stammer out as she strolls over to the desk. She plucks out a sheet of poster board and looks back at me. She winks, and that wink is so powerful I swear I hear a crash of thunder as her eye closes.

Is . . . Kelsey flirting with me? Kelsey fucking Nicolau? No. No way.

And even if she is, it's me and Frankie still. Me and her. I can't let this little crush get the best of me here.

My heart is going wild. My God. I clear my throat, shake my head, and try to focus on the work in front of us.

Everyone comes alive under Frankie's directions, fussing over the poster boards, passing around markers, cutting out letters. It reminds me of being a kid—a little one, really—doing arts and crafts at sleepaway camp years ago. Sharing glue and glitter and wildly awkward first kisses with girls who were just as puzzled as I was about these strange feelings our parents didn't understand. Girls who grew up looking way cooler than me, walking, talking memories that I see living their lives on Instagram. Or in person, like with Kelsey. Most of them are out loud in a way I don't think I'll get to be until I get away from Connecticut.

Well, from my mom, really.

Most of them look and act like Kelsey, who is still here, who is just herself all the time. God, what must it be like? She looks up at me while tracing out some kind of lettering on a board and gives me another smirk that threatens to just ruin my life.

Now is not the time.

The classroom door swings open again, and in walks that new kid.

Phoenix something.

The boy who was falling all over himself to talk to Frankie the other day and seems to be all over her on social media, liking and commenting on every damn thing.

He looks about the room, puzzled, like a new puppy who isn't sure of its surroundings, until he lays eyes on Frankie, and he just lights up. Frankie glances up and spots him, smiling, and there's this sudden twinge of . . .

jealousy, maybe, twisting itself in my chest. It's the way he looks at her and that little smile she flashed back.

It looks way too much like the smile she saves for me. Or the way Kelsey keeps throwing me these playful glances. Like there's something there, hidden and unspoken, waiting to be brought to the surface.

I stroll over to Phoenix.

"Hey." I put my hand out. "You here for SMAAC?"

"Uh, yeah," he says, shaking my hand but not quite looking at me. He tries to peer around me, toward Frankie. "I'm Phoenix."

"Jo," I say, sucking at my teeth. "You're that new kid, right?"

"That's me." He shrugs. "Is, uh . . ." He points over at Frankie. "I'm just gonna check in with Frankie. Are you guys all done already?"

"No, no," I say as he steps around me, walking toward her. "We're not done."

"Great." He grins. "I just wanna do my part, you know?"

"Yeah." I nod.

Phoenix walks over to Frankie, and the two of them chat with each other in hushed voices, and she . . . giggles. Frankie doesn't giggle. I grab a piece of poster board and some markers and make my way over to an empty desk. For a minute, I think about sitting with Kelsey, but this isn't the time to be petty. It's nothing, it's got to be nothing.

It *has* to be nothing.

I don't know if my heart could handle it being something.

· · ·

Kelsey, Lily, and the rest of the surprising new SMAAC crew make their way out of the classroom as the bell rings, signaling lunch for some of us, class for the others. My stomach rumbles at the thought of whatever might be on the Monday cafeteria menu, with a little wave of nausea in my chest. I'm not sure if it's because I'm hungry or because I'm feeling . . . this looming sense of unease.

Phoenix is still lingering in the room, picking up scraps of paper and other supplies, while Frankie fusses over something on her phone at the desk. I debate leaving, but instead I lurk in the classroom, watching as he dumps out the trash and places some collected markers and scissors on Frankie's desk.

This is ridiculous. What is wrong with me? I'm tumbling over my words whenever Kelsey is around, and still, here I am, getting jealous over Frankie having a new friend who clearly has a crush on her. But she seems to be . . . entertaining it? I keep brushing off whatever is happening with Kelsey, but Frankie does not seem to be doing the same.

Ugh, I hate this.

"So . . ." Phoenix says, looking a little coy. "See you later?"

"Yeah, totally." Frankie looks up at him, a little smile on her face.

And with that, he hands her something and ducks out the door. He gives me a second look, and I try to soften my glare at him, but I don't think it works. Besides, I'm not sure I want to pull any of that back.

What is going on here?

"So." I clear my throat. "What is all that?"

"What's what?" Frankie asks, her eyes flitting up from her phone to me and then back down. "I'm working on an event page for the rally."

"You know that's not what I'm talking about, right?" I edge up closer to the desk and she scowls at me.

"I . . . don't?" She gives me a look.

"It's that fuckboy who just went out of here," I snap, but there's something else brewing under all of this, and I have to bite at my lip to stop a sob from wrenching out of me. Not Frankie. Not all this. Between the shit at home and everything going on here, she's all I have. The one safe haven in this disaster town. "Just be honest. If you're about to break my heart just do it."

"What's your problem?" Frankie asks, putting her phone down on the desk. "He's just here trying to help."

"Right," I huff. "I see the way he looks at you. It's the same way he was swooning over you in the hallway the other day. Are you . . . into him?"

"Are you serious, Jo?" Frankie scoffs. "You're jealous? Of what? Also, I'm not sure this is the best place for any of that. You do know what we're here for, right?"

"Fine." I clear my throat, rubbing my forehead. She's right. We're here planning a rally. "I guess I'm overreacting. I'm sorry. All this is just . . . it's a lot."

"It's you and me," Frankie says, getting up and walking

around the desk. She grabs my hands, and it's again taking everything in me not to cry. Over on the desk is the thing Phoenix handed her. It's a folded note with a little heart on it, colored in with red pen, and her name scrawled in the middle.

It is something, but I look away.

I clear my throat.

"Me and you."

Dear Frankie,

My God. You're so much braver than anyone gives you credit for.

I know I haven't been in town long. But I've been here long enough to understand the people here. How everyone seems to bury their head in the sand when dealing with confrontation. When something uncomfortable is in front of them. Everyone at school is talking about Bella, but no one is actually saying anything.

No one is chiming in to take action, to do something about this.

No one but you. And I want you to know that even though you might think no one sees it, that I do. I remember what we talked about that night at the park. How you wrestle with being seen, being heard, being understood.

I get you, Frankie Healy.

And in a new city, where I find myself mostly alone . . . I think you get me too.

Phoenix

P.S: Meet me at the park after school?

Chapter Fourteen

Nick

I stare at the doors to the high school gym for a beat, as a few kids shuffle by me, pushing through. I can hear the roar of what sounds like the entire student body inside as they swing open, a gust of hot air blowing through as the large doors shut.

I don't want to go in there.

All day, everyone has been staring at me. I'm Andrew's best friend. I was there at the party. I'm the one who was close with Bella. There's just this . . . bullet list following me around in the shape of everyone staring daggers at me, each point a painful jab.

I didn't do anything.

And at the same time . . .

. . . that's the problem.

I hear Principal Clarke talking inside. "Okay, okay. Let's all settle down . . ."

Shit.

I nudge the doors open, pushing them as gently as I can

to avoid the usual loud clap sound of the lock and bar, and hold them as they shut behind me. Students are still muttering in the bleachers as Principal Clarke asks everyone to quiet down again. I slide onto an end seat on the bleachers, the closest to the edge and the door. I don't want to walk across the gym in front of everyone. I don't have it in me to find a seat next to anyone I know right now.

I glance up and, in the crowd of kids, spot Lily.

She gives me the finger, and I turn away.

"Thank you, thank you," Principal Clarke says, the talking softening to a din of whispers, sneakers squeaking against the varnished bleachers as people fidget and move. "I know none of you really want to be here right now and that mandatory assemblies aren't exactly the most thrilling way to spend the last class at the end of the day."

"True!" someone shouts. Laughter erupts.

"Okay, okay." Principal Clarke casts sideways glances at the teachers sitting near him. His podium is in front of the bleachers, a couple of feet away, with a few folding metal chairs next to him. Some of the teachers there are familiar: Mr. Martinho, Miss Rishi, Miss Vicente. There are two other people there, looking stern and serious, both holding cups of coffee even though it's, like, 2:00 P.M.

They look like plainclothes police officers. Like they're straight out of a *True Detective* episode, dressed regular, but not regular enough. In a way that says "I'm not a cop!" but just points out that they are. At some point do police officers, like, forget how normal people dress?

I don't know.

But they make me nervous.

"It's been . . . a weekend," Principal Clarke starts, nodding, his tone a bit solemn. "For our community here. Your friends, your parents, your teachers, have been swept up in the . . . well, I almost called it a 'scandal,' but it's not really that, is it? A scandal, a rumor, a bit of gossip—that's something else altogether, reserved for those of you who watch reality television. Where the problems aren't really problems, but jokes."

He sighs, shakes his head, and gives the podium a rap with his knuckle.

"This. This is not a joke." He looks around the bleachers, and it's like he's making eye contact with absolutely everyone. I don't think anybody moves. The silence is intense. He's . . . good at his job.

"A crime was committed here," he continues. "That photo, the one circulating of someone in our community? Not only is that evidence of a crime, but it's also a crime, just sharing that picture. And all of you, as teenagers, as young adults, should absolutely know better. I'm not here to chastise you but to educate. To let you know that your actions have consequences."

I look over my shoulder, at Lily and her friends, some girls I don't really know. They're staring at me. Lily nudges someone in front of her and nods in my direction, this other person's eyes joining theirs.

Goddamn it.

"If any of you are caught continuing to spread that photo, you will be investigated. We aren't talking about detention or suspension. We're talking about expulsion. It is considered an act of violence against one of your peers, regardless of how you might feel about it." He looks over at the we're-totally-not-cops, who nod at him. "Now, Detective Phil Cabarle is going to speak to you a little bit more. But this is a warning coming from me. Do not share that photo. And if you know something about who took the initial photo or anything else that happened that night, you need to do the right thing and speak up."

I swallow, my throat going dry.

Bits and pieces of that night have been working their way back to me. It wasn't just Andrew lurking around Bella, it was him actively nudging everyone else away from her. I can see it now, those moments. Like little pieces of a puzzle I've found on the floor.

But still, I don't think any of that is enough to really help.

And getting involved . . . I don't know if I can do it.

What would Mom say?

I look over my shoulder again, and this time, Lily is glaring at me along with what looks like a third of the bleachers. Everyone on her side is staring down at me, whispering to one another. A flash of heat pulses through me, and I turn away, my eyes fighting to look back.

"Hello, students of Greenport High School, thank you for having me here. I'll try not to take up too much of your time," Detective Cabarle says, taking off his hat. He definitely has that grizzled look of someone who has seen a lot, which is strange considering we're in Greenport, where the most violent things that go on are . . .

Hm.

I guess making a joke about toilet papering trees doesn't really work anymore, when actual violence has happened.

"This is now an active investigation," the detective continues. "If any of you know anything about the events of Saturday night, please don't hesitate to contact the local police department and ask straightaway for me. Or, if you're not comfortable with that, please talk to your principal here or your parents. There are a lot of avenues you can use to get your information to us. We want you to feel safe and to help us make your community a safe one."

He clears his throat.

"But make no mistake." His eyes flit up, looking at everyone again, but his gaze is a lot different from our principal's. There's a fierceness there. "We will get to the bottom of this. We've already talked to the victim, as you can imagine, as well as the accused. You likely won't see them here, and I would ask you to respect their need for privacy in this time. That goes for both of them. I know you might feel this urge to say something on social media, text someone, maybe be . . . not nice, to either of them. What's important here is getting answers, and getting them soon, by not doing anything rash."

I look over my shoulder again, and there's Lily making eye contact with me. She nudges someone next to her, and again, the eyes glance my way. So many. It feels like everyone.

It . . . it feels like everybody here is looking right at me.

Something seizes in my chest, and suddenly it's hard to breathe.

Everything is fucked.

My throat goes wildly dry, and I can't swallow. I feel like I'm choking on air.

I slide off the bleacher and burst through the doors, hurrying into the hallway. I lean over a drinking fountain, and before I can get any water, I start dry heaving. I hold on to the steel frame of it, my body shaking, shaking, until it stops.

I take a few sips of water, my throat absolutely burning.

And when I stand back up, Principal Clarke and Detective Cabarle are right next to me.

"Nick," Principal Clarke says. "Let's . . . take a walk."

"No, no, Principal Clarke. I . . . I didn't . . ." I glance at the detective, who is looking at me intensely. Like he's dissecting everything I say. "I'm just . . ."

"Nick, you're not in trouble," Principal Clarke says. "But I know . . ." He looks at the detective, who just nods back at him. "I know you and Andrew are friends. Everyone knows. You two are inseparable. If you know anything about what happened that night, you need to go to the police with your parents and say something."

I glance at the detective.

"I'm not going to take you in a room and grill you with

questions, kid." A little smirk dances across his face. "But if you don't talk to your parents about this . . . I'll talk to them first."

"I need to think," I say, feeling like I'm about to start sweating.

"And that's okay," Detective Cabarle says, pulling a business card out of his pocket. He hands it to me, and I take it. "When you're ready to talk, have your parents reach out. It's okay. I'm just here to help. But don't take too long."

I look up at Principal Clarke, who nods.

"Okay."

Chapter Fifteen

Phoenix

I smile at the nurse sitting behind the waiting room desk and tap my fingers against the hard particleboard surface. She glances up, her eyes warm.

"If it isn't the world's best younger brother." She beams at me. "Visiting?"

"Hey, Mary." I smile back.

"You know the room," she says, looking back at her computer. "She should be awake."

"Any, you know, updates?" I ask. Her smile shrinks back a little, a tight one full of pity, and I wince. "Okay, okay."

"Sorry, darling," she says. "Let us know if you need anything, she needs anything, the usual."

I walk by the desk in Ruby's ward, a few other nurses nodding at me as I stroll by. We haven't been here that long, but apparently our family has made an impression. Mom showing up almost every other day with pizza for everyone certainly helped, and so does being kind, I think.

Out of the several days I've been coming here, I've seen a lot of yelling and screaming at that desk.

I get it. People are hurting. They want answers. But I'm never sure what shouting at the people who are trying to help (and not getting paid nearly enough to do so) does for anybody. I nearly reach Ruby's room when my heart practically seizes in my chest at the sight of the one next to hers. It's got a yellow square on it.

I walk toward the door; the window looking inside is covered with a curtain.

I brush my fingers over the door and onto the plastic yellow square and sigh.

When we toured the facility, they told us what some of the squares meant. It's something they do in the maternity wards too. Green, surgery. Blue, cleaning. Yellow . . .

. . . means someone died.

I look back down the hall, then toward Ruby's room right next door, and I wonder what the family of the person in that room is like. Are they like us? Is there a brother, like me, just trying his best despite . . . everything telling him none of it is going to be enough?

I search my memory, trying to recall the person in that room. I always just hurried toward Ruby, sometimes catching a quick glimpse of somebody in these other nooks. But nothing I can hold on to.

I hope someone is holding on to whoever was in there as best they can.

I try to steel myself and head into Ruby's room. The door is open, there's no colored square, and she's sitting up in her bed, glaring at the television across from her. She's got her phone in her hand. I walk in, the whole space smelling weirdly clean the way hospitals do, with a hefty splash of flowers, as there are vases of them scattered all about thanks to Mom and her friends back home. Bright pink peonies sit in large vases; white baby's breath frame yellow carnations in others. It's like an overly clean florist shop.

I look up at the television. She's watching *Trillions*.

Of course.

"So . . . what's the latest drama here?" I ask, grabbing a wooden chair from the little desk on the other end of the room and sliding it over toward the bed. "Let me guess. Rich guy is mad at the other rich guy?"

"Shut up," she says, waving me off. She coughs a little after that movement and clears her throat. "You know I love this nonsense."

"I feel like if I had all the money these people have, I'd maybe just . . . not hang out with those other people?" I say as I watch an actor scream at another over something on a computer screen.

"You'd be really bad at writing television like this, then." She pauses the show and turns to look at me, smiling warmly. "What's up? What's going on today on the outside?"

"You always say that, like you're a prisoner or something." I roll my eyes.

"I'm not gonna make it on the outside, Phoenix," she says, gritting her teeth, talking like an old-timey criminal.

"Stop," I say, laughing.

There's a quiet beat, and she's just grinning at me.

"So, what's the latest?" she asks. "I've got nothing but time here to kill, kiddo."

"You're two years older than me. The kiddo thing . . . Ugh." I groan. "I mean, not a lot, not for me. The entire school is buzzing over what happened to that girl, Bella."

"Yeah, that's so sad," Ruby says, deflating a bit.

"But we're going to have a rally to support her." I clear my throat. "This, um, this girl I'm a little into, she's organizing it. We're going to hang out tonight. She helped her report it."

"Wow," Ruby says, nodding. "Good for you. Good for her. I hope she gets justice."

"Same."

"Did you want to maybe"—she wiggles her phone and points at the television—"finish an episode or two with me?"

"Of course." I smile and lean back in the wood chair, teetering it on its back legs a little and rocking myself back and forth with the tips of my toes. I have absolutely no idea what's going on, except a lot of people are wearing wildly expensive-looking outfits in lavish New York City apartments, all with these gorgeous wood-paneled interiors. It looks like someone just took a chisel and carved entire rooms out of a massive tree, leaving huge hollow spaces surrounded by wide arches and carefully sculpted frames.

But from what I know from the few episodes I've

watched with her, and the Wikipedia page I read regularly so I'm caught up, it's a show about some high-profile stock-broker people fighting against the common lawmakers in their state. Everyone sabotages everyone else, but also some people are sleeping with each other. I don't know. It makes her happy.

My phone buzzes a few times before I sneak a peek, with Ruby still totally invested in this show.

> Frankie: Hey you. ♥

> Frankie: Same place, right? Say, 8PM?

My heart slams in my chest. She *does* want to see me.

> Me: Absolutely.

"You, uh, okay there?" my sister asks, and I turn to see her staring at me, confused. "You're, like, sweating a little and breathing all heavy, and there isn't even a sex scene going on."

"Jesus, Ruby." I laugh.

"What's wrong?" She nods at my phone.

"Oh." I exhale. "There's, uh, there's this girl."

"At last, here we go. You flew by that detail earlier and I didn't want to pry." She sits up a little bit in her bed, jostling some of the wires connected to her arms and chest about. "Well, that's a lie. Of course I did, but I respect you."

I move to get up and she shakes her head, groaning a little as she gets situated.

"I'm fine. Go."

And I tell her. About that first day of class, with the fountain pen and the poem, all the sneaky looks we've exchanged in the hallways. The planning for this rally, her club. All the text messages we've been sending back and forth. I hold up my hand, the ink still smeared there a little bit, a tiny splotch like a bruise, washing away ever so slowly.

Ruby's smile grows with every tiny story. It's not a lot of story, just a few days of being increasingly smitten with this girl I don't really know but would love to know better.

"Well." She laughs, grabbing her phone. She swipes at something on the screen, and *Trillions* pops back up on the television across the room. "You better get going. I don't want you to miss that hot date."

"I could just stay—" I start.

"Nope." She shakes her head. "You don't get to put your life on pause just because I'm in here." She turns away from the television and looks right at me. "I know that it's kind of on pause anyway, because of all this." She gestures at herself, up and down, like she's showcasing a new jacket and not her hospital bed. "And really, I know it's that way for Mom too. She had her friends back home. Her coworkers that she liked. Her garden and that really weird co-op." She winces, wrinkling her nose.

"The one that gave out all that mineral water that looked like water from the beach," I say. It was all full of silt and sand and little specks of what the person working there said were "vitamins," but I don't think vitamins can swim.

"So gross." She shakes her head. "And I know you left your writing group, your friends, all the places you found comfortable, to be here. If there's one thing I want for you, right now, it's to be a little more selfish, Phoenix. Think about what you really want."

I look out the hospital room's window. You can see the park from here, a little bit of it anyway, a large patch of trees in the middle of the town.

"Helping take care of you, and helping Mom with all of it, is what I want," I say, looking back to Ruby, who sucks at her teeth. "It's true. I love you guys. I've got no regrets."

"All right." She clears her throat, which sends her into a slight coughing fit. I walk up next to her, this urgent feeling of wanting to help balled up in my chest, but she just holds her hand out toward me, motioning for me to wait. And when it passes, she takes several deep breaths.

She looks at me, her eyes watery from all the coughing.

"Need me to get the nurse?" I ask. "I can buzz for Mary."

"It's fine," she says, her voice a little raspy. "I want you to have fun tonight, and just make the most of our time here, kiddo. Things are hard, but a real Vargas doesn't run when things get hard. Unless you're running toward something. Not away."

I look back out the window and then back at her.

"Go see your girl, go fight for justice." She smiles and tilts her head toward the door to the room. "I'm proud of you."

. . .

Oh.

She's actually here. She came.

Frankie Healy is twisting around on a swing in Poston Park, staring at her phone, as I walk across the large field we ran across just a few days ago. After ditching the now infamous party at that kid Andrew's house. A whole bunch of people I don't know, with last names that escape me, all wrapped up in something horrible.

It's just as cold as it was that night, but I'm feeling a little warmer as I get closer, despite everything going on. Ruby's push was something I really needed. I don't even think I realized how bad I needed it. And I've got some pasta sitting on the countertop at home, with a little container full of sauce, waiting for Mom.

The night is mine.

I clear my throat as I get closer, and she looks up at me, a smile lighting up her face, which is already illuminated from her phone's screen. She tucks the phone away inside her military-style jacket, the dark green making her brown eyes flash.

"Hey," she says, swinging a little, a coy smile on her face.

"Hey yourself."

I get to her and stand in front of the swing.

"How was today?" I ask, and her eyes shift downward at her hands. I reach out and grab them, like she was about to drop them. "It's okay. You can talk to me about it."

She snorts out a laugh and shakes her head.

"I mean, what is there to say?" she grumbles. "It feels like everyone at school is talking about it, but not *really* talking about it. Bella's a rumor, a whisper, a warning. She's not the cool girl in the leather jacket to them anymore, she's just . . . this single photo on social media. That's what they've made her into. A snapshot."

She grits her teeth and huffs, frustrated.

"How do you change that? How do you fix it?" She shakes the chains on the swing as she talks. "We had that painful assembly with the principal and those cops, and everyone was just staring at Nick . . ." She groans. "You know I haven't even seen him at home? He's been avoiding me, coming home wildly late last night and leaving super early this morning. Won't answer my texts. What am I supposed to do?"

"I wish I had an answer," I say, and then my phone buzzes in my pocket. "Just a second."

Mom: Hey sweetheart, what's the plan tonight?

Me: Out with a friend, but I should be back for our show.

Mom: Alright, don't make me watch it without you.

Mom: You text or call your sister today?

Yeah, not sure I do either, Mom.

"All right." I smile, putting my phone away. "I'm all yours."

"Oh?" She smirks.

"Oh!" I gasp, and laugh. "That sounded different in my head."

"You know, you're the best listener that I've ever met." She reaches out and squeezes my hands. "Why don't we just go for a walk? I just need to . . . clear my head of all this."

She hops off the swing, and my hands are still in hers. It's been only a few days of talking to her, of exchanging quick glances in the hallways and awkward texts and passed notes, yet I am so wildly smitten with this girl that I will just follow her anywhere. A random park in the middle of the night, a party full of dangerous strangers, wherever she wants to take me next.

"Let's go."

We walk out of the park, down a path that leads into a section of town that feels a little more city-like, with small shops and boutiques slowly appearing as cute Cape

181

Cod–style houses fade back closer to the park and trees. Frankie starts pointing out, completely unprompted, different places as downtown becomes a lot clearer. An old house that serves as the town museum, some restaurants with outdoor seating for maybe three people, a candle shop that's as narrow as a candle . . . as if this town tries to squeeze big ideas into tiny spaces everywhere. I haven't been through this section of town since our initial move and the few times Mom dropped me off at school. Everything just zipped by in a quick blur of storefront windows and sign fonts, not in a way I could latch on to. It's like that first day at the new school, where faces just disappeared as quickly as I saw them.

I glance over at Frankie.

Well. Except one.

We slow down at a vintage clothing shop where, she tells me, she finds all her jackets and a lot of her clothes. There's a mannequin wearing some kind of bizarre Civil War–looking outfit. I scowl at it, trying to get a handle on what I'm seeing.

"There are some Civil War reenactors in town," she says derisively, as we stop in front of the window. "Connecticut was a pretty big deal then, you know."

"I didn't."

"If you went to Greenport Middle School, it was impossible *not* to know that." She steps toward the window and peers down at some of the trinkets on the sill inside. I squint and realize there are some buttons and what look like medals and ribbons. "It's a big thing at the high school too."

"Are those real?" I ask.

"Might be," she says. "You'd have to ask Mr. Martinho. I don't know if you've met him yet, the history teacher who lets us use his classroom?" She glances back up at me. "He's . . . I don't know, something in the reenactment battalion. General? A bunch of us, his students, attend his big event every spring."

"Is that . . . a fun thing?"

"God no." She laughs. Oof, her laugh. It's this airy, bright thing that sweeps me up, like a song I want on repeat. "But you know, he goes out of his way for us, Mr. Martinho. And when people show up for you, you show up for them."

"I like that."

"I like you." She smirks and gives me a little nudge before continuing along the sidewalk. She's already won me over, head over feet. With her strength and bravery and wild honesty. We walk by a pastry shop, the smell of sugar and butter floating through the air so thick that I'm convinced the scent will turn into one of those smoke arms and hands in old cartoons and carry me in. Right next door is a coffee shop that looks unbelievably cozy. I can see the warm earth tones of the furniture from the large glass window, beckoning, looking all the more snug with the growing chill of evening.

"This place looks amazing," I say, slowing down a little. She stops and nods. I should have come here to chat with my writing group, instead of that other place across town. I wonder if they can make a London Fog here too.

"Me and Jo come here every Sunday, after she wraps up church."

"Jo's that girl from your club, right?" I ask.

"Oh," Frankie says, like she's just caught herself. "Yeah."

"She's got . . . a lot of energy?" I venture, not sure what to say about the girl who seemed so wildly furious to see me. Frankie keeps walking. "What's her story?"

"She has . . . complicated parents, just like me. Just like you, I guess." She lets out a laugh. "Like every kid in our high school, I imagine, honestly. They don't like her being out and proud."

"Oh, that's awful." I suck at my teeth.

She glances up at me. "You think so?"

"Well, yeah, of course," I say.

Frankie smiles a little and keeps walking, pointing out other places. And I wonder if I should have asked her something there and then. But that's . . . not something that's mine to ask, but . . . how do I navigate all this? There was something more behind that "you think so?" but I don't think I should pry. If she has something she wants to tell me there, she can when she's ready.

Although . . .

It might explain why that Jo girl seemed to hate me immediately. And I wonder if she and Frankie are . . . something. Am I getting in the way? Should I be here now, plotting out ways to hold her hand and looking for a place to steal a kiss?

We keep strolling and a used bookshop tempts the hell out of me, and we slow down at the entrance, large metal shelves on wheels outside, a sign advertising dollar paperbacks.

"Planning to rummage?" she asks, leaning against one of the shelves. The metal squeaks a little as it juts out just a bit, and she giggles in surprise. "See anything you're into?"

I just stare at her. "I do."

"Shut up." She rolls her eyes, but smiles warmly, and starts flipping through the books on her side of the shelf. The door to the bookshop chimes and swings open, and a young woman peeks out. Her jacket is a bit like Frankie's, with enamel pins all over it instead of patches.

"Hey, kids, we're closing in, like, fifteen, okay?" Her eyes settle on Frankie. "Oh! Hey, Frankie."

"Hi, Dahlia." Frankie peers up from the shelves, smiling still. "We won't keep you."

"No rush," the bookseller says, darting back inside.

"Do you just know *everyone*?" I ask, plucking out a beat-up and well-loved copy of a Richard Russo novel, and thumb through looking for others. All the paperbacks here look just as weathered, like they've seen countless hands, traveling here from who knows how far. I run my hand over the spines, quickly looking over the names, a collection of literary fiction, sci-fi and fantasy, poetry. Ted Chiang, Jonathan Lethem, John Scalzi, Maggie Smith, Zora Neale Hurston. I spot a few favorites of my friends in the writing group back home and wonder where the post office in this town is. It'd be nice to send them a care package full of reads.

"I feel like every time I'm around you . . ." I say, patting the top of some books. I feel a lot of things when I'm around Frankie, that's for sure. ". . . folks just swarm your way."

"Eh, not really." She shrugs. "I just keep bringing you to places where that happens, where I'm comfortable, so I look cool. My club, a bookstore I like, my favorite vintage shop—"

"That party doesn't count, does it?" I ask, finding another book, a Michael Chabon novel with deckle edges. Ruby loves him. The latest novella from Neil P. Bardhan too, with a whole bunch of poker chips on the cover. I'm not sure if she's read either of these, but for a dollar apiece, I can risk scooping them up as a surprise to bring to the hospital. Anything to get her away from that depressing rich-people show.

"No," she scoffs. "I only went for . . ." She pauses and looks up at me from over the steel bookshelf. "Well, for you, if I'm being honest with myself. And as an olive branch to my brother, which I now regret. I thought you'd want to meet people, you know? Help you feel a little less alone here."

"Well, we didn't exactly stay for any of that to happen." I smile, and she smirks back. "I'm glad we didn't, though. And I'm glad you thought of me. I mean, you barely know me."

"I want to, though." She ducks back into the shelf. "This counts as getting to know you. Books are a great way to figure out what someone's deal is."

I spot a dark green spine and a familiar typeface and reach down to the bottom of the shelf. I feel a little rush of excitement and hold the book up.

"Isn't this the book you love?" I ask, holding out a copy of *Great Expectations*. "It's in better shape than the one you've been carrying around."

She looks over and her eyes go wide.

"No way." She beams, taking the book from my hands. "I love these editions. They do all these pretty fonts on the cover and just . . ." She looks at me again. "Thanks for finding this." She turns and walks around the shelf, giving me a quick kiss on the cheek, and moves to open the door to the bookshop.

It rattles in her hand, closed and locked.

"Ugh," she grumbles, and taps on the door. "Dahlia!"

A few latches unlock the door, and the bookseller peeks her head out, surprised to still see us.

"Oh!" Her eyes settle on the book in Frankie's hand and the few under my arm. She waves us off. "Just take them, you two. Just make sure you post about it on social media or bring another unfamiliar face in. That'll do."

"What?!" Frankie exclaims, holding the book to her chest. "Thank you!"

"Thanks!" I shout, waving the three books at her in my hand.

"Any time." Dahlia smiles and ducks back inside the shop.

Frankie practically skips away from the store, the book under her arm. She looks at me, her face just full of joy, and nods at the books in my hand.

"All right, well, speaking of. What's the deal with those?" she asks. "What do those books tell me about you, Phoenix Vargas?"

"Oh. Maybe nothing? Mom loves Richard Russo." I look down at the books. "He writes these, like, big family comedy dramas. I don't know. I think she sometimes wishes our family was a bit more like these or the ones on television, big and sprawling with way too many cousins and siblings and the like. But it's just us."

"That's . . . a bit sad," Frankie says, and we start walking. It's definitely getting colder out, and the lights in a handful of the storefronts on the block are slowly flickering off. We stop just under a streetlight, the lamp washing us in a yellow-orange glow, like a spotlight. Frankie stops and stares up at it, then right at me.

"What about the other ones?" She shifts the copy of *Great Expectations* under her other arm and takes my hand.

"Oh, they're for Ruby, my sister." I look back, as though I can see the bookstore and shelves from where we are. I'll have to visit that bookstore again, when I can really dig in. "She really likes weird books and, like, alternate histories. Chabon and Bardhan write those. Says there's . . . hope in all that."

"Hope?" Frankie asks.

"Yeah, you know." I exhale. "Rewriting history in a way where good things happen instead of bad. Although I feel like most alternate history stories tend to make things worse. But it's the idea that you can . . . still live another life, possibly, on another timeline someone has written for you."

"Is that what you'll do?" Frankie asks. "Write stories about your sister?"

"I hope not," I say.

"Why?"

"Because." I swallow. "If I'm writing an alternate history for her, it means she isn't here anymore." I bite at my lip. "I went to see her before we met up and it never gets any easier."

"Well, I think I know what your books say about you, Phoenix Vargas," she says, wiping a tear away from my cheek with a thumb.

"And what's that?"

"That maybe you care a little too much." Frankie smiles. "And anyone on the receiving end of all that is incredibly lucky."

We stand there for a beat, and I feel like I can't turn away from her. I make myself push past it and take her hand again.

"And what about you?" I ask, as we walk hand in hand up this main street. My heart is slamming in my rib cage. Whatever this is, whatever is happening here, I don't want to mess it up. What do I have to do so she stays? So *this* stays. I remember Mom pleading with my dad when Ruby was in the hospital back home to not leave. To stick it through with us. All while I sat there in the living room, unable to move. Forced to just listen as my family unraveled.

Nothing she said could change his mind.

He looked down at me, his expression defeated and crushed, and walked out the door with only a duffel bag.

"What do you mean?" she asks.

"The book." I point my chin at it, still clutched in her hand. "What's with Charles Dickens? Of every author out there to be your thing, why him?"

"Oh." She laughs. "I don't know if it's *him*. It's definitely not him. Not some old dead white guy writer, even if he was progressive for his time. For someone who wrote about people fighting back against oppressive powers, he sure didn't paint marginalized people in the best light."

"So . . . he was racist?" I ask.

"Yeah, not great, that guy," she huffs, then stops. "But . . . Estella, in *Great Expectations*. I don't know, she's this adopted girl raised by a woman who tries so hard to shape her into someone she's not. And I think in all the movies and adaptations Estella gets painted to be this . . . villain, because of it. This girl who was just carefully crafted by someone else. Nurture, if that's even the word for it, instead of nature."

She glances up at me.

"I'm like Estella, in a lot of ways. Born to people who didn't really care for me, raised by people who want me to be someone else completely. And everyone around me is indifferent to that hurt I carry around, and I'm just . . . so frustrated by the apathy."

She sighs and looks up the street, her eyes searching for someone far away.

"And before you do that thing where you ask about my birth parents, as most people do when I get on a tear like that, no, I haven't met them. I don't know a thing about them. And I'm really not ready to." She glances at me. "Just . . . sorry. It's a touchy thing and it always comes up. It's always a question."

I swallow. "There's nothing I can say here. Or ask." I take a step toward her. "But I can listen. That's what I do. It's what I'm good at." I take one of her hands, and she looks back at me, her eyes a little watery. "And I hear you. You're heard."

"That's all I really want."

She steps toward me and lifts a hand up to my face, cupping my cheek. I close my eyes, exhaling, and open them to see her staring right at me. Those brown eyes, just digging right through me. Seeing right through me.

She tilts her head up a little and whispers, "Is this okay?"

"Yeah." I clear my throat. "Yeah, definitely."

And she kisses me, under a streetlight, with books that say so much about who we are and what we want tucked under our arms. Stories of families, of relationships, of dashed dreams, clinging to us the way gossip seems to stick in this town, a burden in our hearts.

I cup her face in both of my hands, and she kisses me deeper.

And the books fall to the ground.

• • •

"Shh." Frankie giggles as the front door to her house creaks open.

"I don't think this is a good—" I start, but she pushes me against the doorframe and kisses me again. "Okay, let's go."

I'm not sure what I expected inside Frankie's home; the light gray house with fancy stonework on bits of the exterior, including one of those elaborate, round-looking, castle-like rooms off to the side, looks like something straight out of a wholesome rich-family sitcom. Big glass windows with thick white window frames, wooden shutters that look like they're older than the actual house . . . a lot of love and effort went into this place.

But the inside. All this reclaimed and repurposed furniture. Even someone like me who doesn't know a thing about furniture—because why would I?—can tell that's what all this is. A coffee table that looks like it's made from an old door, bookshelves made of different-colored wood, stone slabs making up bits of the kitchen that appear to be from somewhere else entirely . . . it's wild and beautiful.

And I can't help but wonder what her parents' obsession with giving forgotten things a home is. And how that feels for Frankie. It's painfully on the nose.

"Come on," Frankie says, pulling me away from the living room and the hall opening to the kitchen. I follow her up the stairs.

"Is anyone home?" I ask, whispering a little.

"Who cares?" she scoffs, and I keep walking with her, careful on each squeaky step.

"Wait, no, really." I stop on the steps, peering up

toward the second floor and back down the staircase. "I don't want you to get in trouble."

"It's fine," she insists. "My mom is who knows where, and my dad is always working. Nick is out being Nick and avoiding facing what he's done. Or didn't do. Both. We've got this whole house, and I've got all of you to myself."

"Did you lock the front door?" I ask, peering back downstairs again.

"Please." She laughs. "This is Greenport. No one locks their doors."

We walk into her bedroom.

"But we're gonna lock mine."

Bella: Hey are we meeting up tomorrow to talk about the rally this week?

Bella: I'm . . . a little scared here, you guys.

Bella: My mom keeps crumbling into pieces every time she looks at me, and my dad just wanders around the house like he's going to dig a trench in the floorboards with his feet. He's so angry. Wants to go beat up Andrew's dad.

Bella: I feel like I'm in first grade again. My dad can beat up your dad, only it's real and less funny.

Jo: Jesus.

Jo: I'm sorry.

Jo: Yeah, let's meet up tomorrow. Maybe your house? Or Frankie's?

Jo: Frankie you in? You're awfully quiet over there.

Bella: Hello?

Jo: Frankie, I'm sorry about freaking out at the meeting today. Don't take it out on the group.

Bella: Freak out?

Jo: I . . . got jealous over Phoenix. I'm not proud.

Bella: Oh, Jo.

Bella: You're perfect. You don't have anything to worry about. Frankie'll agree.

Bella: Right Frankie?

Bella: Responding would be great.

Chapter Sixteen

From the street I can see the light is on in Frankie's room, and there's a car in the driveway. I wonder if her dad is there. Or Nick. He's been missing in action since everything went down. I haven't even seen a glimmer of him in the school hallways or on social media during all of this. Apparently, he was at the big assembly but ran out. I couldn't see him, but everyone is talking about it.

Whatever the case, I feel like I'm stepping into a mess.

But Frankie isn't answering my texts, and I definitely melted down over nothing. This is at least one disaster I can clean up by apologizing.

I walk inside the back door and catch her mom and dad sitting at the kitchen table, quietly reading something. Notes about who knows what. Letters, maybe? Bills?

"Hey, Mr. and Mrs. Healy," I say, walking into the living room. Her dad perks up, her mom's back still toward me, and waves, pointing at me.

"Hey, Jo," he says, and then his face turns up, confused. "Wait, I thought you were here already." He glances up toward the ceiling like he can maybe see through the second floor. "Huh. Well, Frankie's upstairs. I thought you two were up there."

He looks over to Frankie's mom.

"MJ?" he ventures. "Jo is here. Do you want to say hi?"

"Hm?" Frankie's mom mutters, and turns around. She looks completely out of it, moving like she's a character in a slow-motion scene in one of those way-too-long Zack Snyder movies Nick used to make us watch. "Oh. Hey, Jo." She turns back around to Frankie's dad, who looks so wildly frustrated he might explode.

"Jesus, MJ." He shakes his head and goes back to looking at the papers in front of him. "Can you at least wait until the kids are asleep before hitting the bottle?"

"Don't!" Mrs. Healy slams a hand on the table, knocking a glass over. I shrink back, even though I'm nowhere near them. She scrambles for it and Mr. Healy gets up, and that just . . . feels like my cue to get out of here. I hurry toward the stairs, the sounds of Frankie's parents starting to argue behind me as I make my way to her room. It feels like the smallest things set those two off, and I don't want to be that thing any more than it seems I already am.

I get enough of that at home.

I reach Frankie's bedroom and try to open the door, but it's locked.

"Go away!" Frankie shouts from inside, but she's . . . giggling. The sound of rustling around and bedsprings leave me puzzled, and I knock on the door again. "Just a . . ." More laughter. "Just a second, Jesus."

That giggle. It's the same one from the meeting when—

The door swings open.

And I step back.

It's Phoenix.

"Oh, hey." He smiles, swinging the door open wide. Frankie is sitting there on her bed, her hair tousled, a book in her hands. She looks up at me, and her face drops.

"Jo." She straightens up, clinging to that book.

"It's upside down," I say, barely getting the words out.

"What?" she asks.

"That book," I say, clearing my throat. "The one you're pretending to read. It's upside down."

She looks at the book and up at me, before putting it aside. I scowl at it.

Who the hell is Richard Russo?

"Jo, it's not what—"

"Hey, wait. Don't we have biology class together?" Phoenix asks, tilting his head. "I know we met at the club, but we also know each other from there, right?" He's like a golden retriever and has no idea what's going on right now in front of him.

"Yeah, our group dissected an earthworm together."

"I knew it." He snaps his fingers. "Frankie showed me your coffee shop today. It was—"

"I'm sorry, there's no way I can do this," I snap, shaking my head.

"Jo, wait!" Frankie shouts.

I bound down the stairs, and in the middle of whatever just happened with Phoenix and Frankie and me, I guess the Healys have resumed their fighting, because they are going at it in the kitchen. I want to rush out, but it's like seeing an accident on the side of the highway, and I can't help but do that rubbernecking thing that slows everyone down. The two of them have been a slow-motion car crash going on for the last half of this year, and the collision feels so imminent.

"You don't get to just say anything in there!" Mrs. Healy shouts, swiping at some of the papers on the table.

"That's the point of therapy!" he yells, grabbing the flying sheets. "And watch it, we need these worksheets—"

"I'm not filling out a bunch of stupid homework. I'm not a child. I don't need to do assignments to figure out what's wrong here." She angrily points between the two of them.

"What's wrong is you've got a problem and don't want to fess up to it," he yells, and then he rushes past her and starts riffling through her purse.

"What—what are you—" she stammers, reaching for the bag.

He pulls out a little orange medicine container full of pills and shakes it at her.

"You think I don't know?!" he yells. "You think I don't know what happens under my own goddamn roof?! Why are you taking these with your wine?! Are you out of your damn mind? I should call your doctor and have them pull your prescription!"

"No! Don't you dare—"

"Hey, so—" I interrupt, and the two of them turn to look at me, shock marring their faces. "You should know that Frankie is upstairs with a boy in her bed."

"What!" her dad says, not so much asks, as he walks toward me and the stairs.

"There's a boy in here?" Her mom does the same, following. "I thought you—"

"No, wasn't us fooling around this time. It's someone else."

Her mom looks at me, sharply. "What do you mean, *us*?"

There's a rustling crash and all of us turn toward the front door and the big glass window that overlooks the Healys' beautifully maintained yard . . . and see Phoenix, climbing awkwardly out of a bush. He brushes himself off, looks right at us in the window, and hauls ass down the street. He's got a bundle of books under one arm, and the other is tugging at his belt buckle. He doesn't even have his shoes on.

"Jo."

I look up at the top of the stairs, and there's Frankie, looking down at me from the second floor. She looks heartbroken.

I make my way out the front door.

I can hear her and her parents screaming at each other for at least a solid block away.

Nick: Hey Andrew.

Nick: I'm coming over.

Nick: Step outside, let's talk.

Mr. Montefiore: Nick, I need you to stop texting my son.

Mr. Montefiore: Everyone is going through a hard time right now, and it's not helping.

Mr. Montefiore: He did nothing wrong, and all of you are just feeding this fire.

Nick: Tell Andrew I'll be parked outside.

Mr. Montefiore: Don't make me call the police, Nick.

Nick: You won't call the police.

Mr. Montefiore: This is harassment.

Nick: I just want to talk.

Mr. Montefiore: Stop it. I won't warn you again, and I won't respond to further messages.

Chapter Seventeen

Frankie

I watch Jo run out into the night, taking the opposite route from Phoenix, the two people I love most in the world literally just running away from me as things get more difficult.

"What the hell is going on, Frankie?" Dad yells. "Who *was* that?"

"Jo?" I wince.

"Don't play games with me," Dad snaps. "Who was the boy that fell off our roof, frantically trying to buckle his belt as he ran across our lawn?!"

"Oh God," Mom moans, her face in her hands. "Was that . . . is this . . . your first time?"

"That's not your business!" I exclaim, shaking my head. "It's my body, I'll do whatever I want."

"Frankie, we're not trying to . . . diminish your agency here, but you're sixteen," Dad says, and I can tell he's desperately trying to appeal to me here. "You're too young, especially with some boy we don't even know. So, I'll ask again, who was that?"

"Phoenix." I clear my throat. "He's . . . new at school."

"So, you don't even know him?!" Mom practically shrieks. Dad shrinks back, grimacing.

"MJ, come on," he says.

"Don't MJ me, Steve!" she shouts. "She's too young to be doing anything with some boy she doesn't even know."

"You know, I'm sorry, but it's crazy to me that you can sit here and have no problem with what happened with Bella and Andrew and Nick—"

"Your brother had nothing to do with—" she yells.

"I don't care!" I shout. "You had no problem with what happened. None. You brushed it off like it was all Bella's fault and tried to tell us not to get involved. Well, we're involved. I'm involved. She didn't get to choose to have sex with someone, but I did. And I do. And not just with Phoenix."

"What are you—" Dad starts.

"Jo," I say, pushing the words out. "I'm bisexual. We've been something for a while now."

"Now you're just deliberately trying to make us upset," Mom says, starting to pace around. "That's all you're doing here. You don't mean any of that."

"Whoa. Whoa now," Dad says. "Okay, let's all just take a breath before someone says something they can't take back. Frankie, I . . . I wish you would have told us." He squats down, looking up at me. "I want you to know that you're loved, you know that, right?"

I can't do this.

I can't deal with this.

"How *would* I know that?!" I snap. "How the hell would I know that, especially from you? You're never here!"

"Well, that's not fair, I have to work—"

"You don't!" I shout. "I know you don't. You could be here, at home. But she drives you away and you don't even fight for us." Phoenix's story of his father and family flash through my mind, how his dad just left when things got difficult. How is this any different?

"Frankie!" Mom yells, and I make my way up the stairs, bolting into my room. I start throwing clothes into one of my backpacks, cramming in as much as I can while scrounging stuff up around my room. Deodorant. Makeup. Hair stuff. I scan for my wallet, a phone charger. An extra battery. My laptop. I push it all down into the bag. Down, down, down.

"What are you doing?!" Mom asks, frantic. She's in my doorway, Dad right behind her.

"None of your business!" I shout.

"It *is* our business," Dad says, inching around Mom. "You're our child, and we love you."

"Am I?!" I glare at them and have to force back a sob from yanking itself from my chest. Not here. Not now. "Look at me. Look. At. Me. That piece of paper you have doesn't make me your kid because you've got it in a file downstairs someplace."

I turn to Mom.

"You thought if you raised me around all these white kids, around you and the rest of the family and Nick, that I'd turn out just like you. Like one of those stupid ornaments on the tree, a—a story in your Christmas cards. Reclaimed like all your furniture. But you only see what you want to see when it comes to me. When it comes to my truth."

"Sweetie . . ." Dad ventures, clearing his throat. "Please, all we've done is love you."

"Right, you're all so wonderful for rescuing me. The poor Black child that you saved. I know you love how woke it makes you look. That's why you adopted me, right?"

"Frankie, no! We wanted a child. We didn't care about the color."

"No kidding." I throw my backpack over my shoulder and push past them and down the stairs. I hear them frantically following. "I'm not a fucking chair."

"Frankie, don't!" Mom shouts.

"It's okay," Dad says. "Let her go. She'll come back, she needs space."

"I told you!" Mom yells. "I didn't want to go to therapy today. I wanted to be home. I didn't want to leave her or Nick or—"

"What are we supposed to do?! Hire a sitter?! They aren't *children* anymore, MJ!"

I fling the door open.

"You weren't there for us," Mom shouts at Dad. "You don't even know us anymore."

"No wonder she fucking hates you," Dad snarls.

And I run off into the evening.

Mom: Frankie.

Mom: Please, just come back home.

Mom: I'm sorry, I'll get better. I'll find a way to be better. To be good.

Mom: Please. Just answer me. Pick up your phone.

Chapter Eighteen

Nick

I'm sitting in my car outside Andrew's house for the second day in a row.

What would I even say to him if he came out? I'm not sure. I don't know what I'd do either. This anger I'm filled with isn't like anything else I've ever held. And despite all my practiced speeches in the car mirror and in the shower at home, it's all got me coming up short. There's nothing I can possibly hammer out of him, with my words or my balled-up shaking fists, that can make things better.

I should be at home, trying to ease the tensions. Not here wrestling with all of mine.

Dad is barely holding it together, Mom is falling apart right in front of us, and Frankie's anger and resentment is the fuse that'll set everything off. And in a lot of ways, I feel like I've become the precarious, lit match to all of that. I keep dancing around them, trying to make everyone happy, trying my best to just . . . smooth it all over, but I think the delay is only making the inevitable explosion worse.

Over the last few days, it's been coming back. Slowly. Pieces of that alcohol-fueled evening. And the more I think of Bella, the more I see it. The more I see her. In Andrew's room, sprawled out on the bed. Him saying that he was going to take care of her, that I didn't have to worry. I was there. Up there in his bedroom, her sleeping on his comforter.

That smile he had on. That awful smile.

And I just . . .

I just left her there.

And the story he's been spinning with me, when we were playing ball outside, it was what he wanted me to believe happened. And he's just going to tell that to anyone who will listen.

There's a flicker of movement inside Andrew's house, by the large front windows, but just as quick as it was there, it's gone.

I think he sees me out here. And I wonder if he's afraid.

Fuck him—good.

I take out my phone and stare down at it. It would be so easy right now, to just call that detective or reach out to the school principal. Just . . . just call them. A few buttons on the phone, a few words, and maybe—just maybe—a lot of this gets fixed. But then how am I protecting everything my family worked for? That I worked for? Is it selfish? Am I wrong? Do I even know what I actually saw—

"Hey!" a voice shouts.

I spot Andrew's dad, standing in the doorway to his home. And he's got a bat in his hand. I reach for my keys and fumble them, the large key ring and kitsch tumbling down by my feet. I bend down and grab them, and just as quickly as he appeared in the doorway of his home, he's looking in at me from the middle of the street, bat pointed at the car like he's signaling where he's about to hit a home run.

"I'm gonna need you and your family to stay away from here," Mr. Montefiore spits out, staring daggers at me. "And you need to stop lurking around in your car. My boy didn't do anything."

"You *know* he did," I say, turning the key in my car. The engine turns over but doesn't start.

A loud crash snaps me back to Andrew's dad. My passenger-side mirror is clean off the car, and he's got his bat slung over his shoulder.

"Get the hell out of here," he snarls.

I turn the key in my car again, it catches, and I head home.

• • •

When I pull up to the house, there's an unexpected scene playing out on the front lawn. Normally no one is ever out there, but there's Mom crying on the front steps, while Dad paces around angrily on the grass, looking down at his phone.

I put the car in park and hop out, hurrying over to them.

"What is it?" I ask. "What's going on?"

"Your sister!" Mom shouts, her hands shaking. Her

cheeks are streaked with tears, and I turn to Dad, who holds up a finger as he finishes typing something out.

"Dad?" I ask. "Is she okay?"

"She's fine, she—"

"You can't know that!" Mom yells at him, getting up from the stairs. She walks over, but she's swaying, like she can't quite catch her balance. She clutches her balled-up hands to her chest. "My baby is out there, *my baby*, and we don't know where she is!"

The way she stresses *my baby*.

It's this guttural wail kind of cry, like nothing I've heard before.

"Mom . . ." I start, taking a step toward her. "Hey."

"Where *were* you?!" she screams, spinning on me. I take a step back. "You're her brother. You're supposed to be here to protect her."

That word. "Protect." It rattles around in my head, shaking me down. Protect Frankie, protect Mom, protect Bella, protect—

"I was just . . ." I clear my throat. "I wanted to talk to Andrew."

"Andrew?!" She runs her hand through her hair, gritting her teeth. "No. No, no, no. I told you not to get involved in any of that. Why would you go see him?"

I look over at Dad, who is texting someone.

"What are you doing?" I ask. He looks up at me, puzzled. "Yeah, Dad, you. What is that? What is happening? Where's Frankie? You can't tell me that you're working right now."

"What? No! That's what I'm trying to find out!" he says defensively. "I've been posting on the neighborhood Facebook group and messaging friends. But your mom keeps carrying on. Frankie took off with a backpack."

"And you just let her walk out!" she yells.

"You're the one who pushed her out, MJ!" he screams back.

"What the hell." I make a beeline back toward my car. I swing the door open and slam it after I climb inside. A piece of the broken mirror rattles off and onto the ground, some slice of metal that probably held something up.

"Where are *you* going now?" Mom hurries over to the car, looking frantic. "You can't leave too, Nick. You can't get involved. Wait, where's your mirror? Never mind. You can't—"

"I can do whatever I want, Mom!" I shout. "What's the worst that's gonna happen, going after Frankie? She's my sister. You didn't want me to help out Bella and look at everything that happened. Everyone is unraveling!"

"But—"

"But nothing! What's Harvard going to say about me looking for my sister? What the hell is wrong with you?!" I start the car and peel it out down the driveway, Mom shouting after me.

Six.

More.

Months.

I don't even have to put the address into my GPS on my phone, I think I know where she headed. It's the only other place I can possibly think of, besides her favorite coffee shop or the school or that bookstore, and it's way too late for any of them to be open. I tear through the neighborhood, rounding around downtown toward the Taylors', and it feels like muscle memory just takes me there. I don't think I've been to Jo's house since we were kids, really. There comes a point in high school when suddenly you're not hanging out with your sister and your sister's friends, and I'm wondering why that is and why I let it happen.

Maybe . . . maybe I shouldn't have let myself get so distant.

Maybe shit like this wouldn't be happening.

I slow down to a stop in front of Jo's house. Her home is the same as I remember it, a modest little one-story ranch with a yard packed full of evergreen shrubs and a slightly ostentatious Virgin Mary shrine. A bunch of flowerless, winter-season rosebushes stand guard around it, and a little water feature stands behind it, no water pouring over anything. Winter and all.

I remember throwing change in that thing when we were little, making wishes, unable to fish the coins out because of the thorns around the statue. You had to make your wishes count.

There were no do-overs.

I get out of the car and slam the door.

To my surprise, the front door to the house opens up slowly, and I spot Mrs. Taylor, her face obscured by the mesh screen door. She smiles curiously and steps outside, her arms crossed.

"Nick," she says, tilting her head a little to the side. "To what do we owe the pleasure?"

"Hi, Mrs. Taylor. Is Jo home?" I ask, trying not to sound too antsy.

"Yeah, just a minute." She ducks inside but peers out at me again, like she's not quite sure I'm really here. And I get it. It's been a while since I ran around their yard and all that. I pull my phone out and fire off a few texts to Frankie:

> **Me:** Hey. What's up? Where are you?

> **Me:** Mom and Dad are losing their minds.

> **Me:** Just let me know if you're okay.

But not so much as a notification that she's typing pops up. No little bubble with little dots. Not even a "read" tag, which means either she isn't looking at her phone, which feels wildly unlikely knowing Frankie, or she's turned those received messages off.

That feels more like her.

"Hey."

I look up from my phone, and there's Jo, arms crossed just like her mom a moment ago. She looks wildly disappointed to see me here.

"Hey, Jo, I—"

"Save it," she says, cold and quick. "You had one chance, you know. To do the right thing. With Bella." She shakes her head. "More than one, apparently. I heard about you bolting at the assembly, the detective right there. All you had to do was stand up for her, report what you saw. Instead, you let her go to the police alone, with just me and Frankie, no other witnesses."

"Jo, no, this isn't about that—"

"Because of your mom?" she scoffs. "How *old* are you, Nick? Not to get all heteronormative here, but be a fucking man."

She glares at me, and I swallow, clearing my throat.

"Are you done?" I ask.

"Yeah, I'm definitely finished. With you, with your whole family. Frankie. I can't believe—"

"Wait, you know?" I ask, taking a step toward her. She scowls. "Where did she go? Is she here? Did she tell you?"

"What are you talking about?" she asks, walking out of the house, closing the door behind her. She stops for a beat, like she's listening for something, and turns to me, speaking a bit softer. "My parents don't know about . . . you know, me and Frankie. About me, sure. Not her. And us. Not that it matters now anyway."

"Why?" I ask.

"We're done," Jo says, a little tremble in her voice. She closes her eyes and bites her lip, shaking her head. "She's sleeping with that Phoenix kid."

"What, really?" I try to remember him from the party and the school halls, but I didn't really get to chat with him much. "Is that where she is?"

"Where she is?"

"Jo, she ran away," I explain. "She got in some massive

fight with my parents and left. She's not answering her phone, not texting, nothing."

"Shit." Jo exhales and runs her hand through her hair. "Where do you think she could have gone?"

"Honestly, here." I shrug and she scowls at me. I almost laugh. "What? Where else would I think she might go? You're her . . . were her . . . I don't know. Do you think she went to that Phoenix kid's house?"

"Maybe?" She paces a little. "I . . . when I caught them in her room together—"

"Wow."

"Yeah . . ." She sniffles. "I, uh, ran down the stairs and maybe . . . maybe outed her to your parents . . ."

"Jesus, Jo."

"I know, I . . ." She crumbles down onto the stoop of her house, her hands in her hair pressed against the sides of her head. "I don't know, I lost it, I . . ."

And now she's crying. I squat down next to her and scoot over onto the steps. I'm . . . not exactly sure what to do here, so I reach my arm around her shoulders, and she presses into me, crying into my chest.

"I love her so much," she sobs, muffled in my jacket. "I kept trying to show her, you know? Every day. All the time. Waiting for her, hiding, holding everything so close to my chest. To keep her safe. I just wanted to keep her safe and love her. And I just let her down. I let everyone down."

"It's okay," I say, and sigh. Her words feel way too close to my own, my own thoughts and attempts and gestures that have all just not done what they were meant to. "Me too."

For a moment, it feels like my phone is burning a hole in my pocket, I'm that aware of it. Jo lets go of me, sniffs loudly. I pull out my cell.

The detective's business card comes out with it, practically stuck to the back.

I stare at it for a beat.

"It's time," Jo says, and I look up to see her staring at me intently. "You waited long enough. You know what you have to do." She gets up, opens the front door, and peers out at me. "And don't think that hug changed anything. That was about Frankie, not you. Make the call."

The door slams behind her as she leaves.

I tap the card against my phone. Waves of nausea rattle my stomach, and I swallow.

I dial.

"Detective Cabarle."

"Um . . . hi." My throat's gone wildly dry and no amount of swallowing or clearing it seems to be helping. "Sorry, excuse me. I'm . . . this is Nick Healy. From the—"

"I know who you are, kid," Detective Cabarle says. "You shouldn't be talking to me without a parent or guardian present. Are you willing to come down to the station with someone?"

"I'm . . . eighteen, sir."

There's a pause on the other end.

"Oh." He huffs. "Okay, well, I guess that changes things. Your principal said you weren't."

"Ah." I nod to myself. "Well, there's a lot of kids there at Greenport."

"Well, Mr. Healy, I would appreciate seeing you down at the precinct as soon as possible. Tomorrow?"

I look out toward my car and, for a moment, wonder how the hell I got here.

"Mr. Healy?"

"Yes," I say, the word rushing out of my mouth. "Yes, I'll be there. I'm ready."

Jo: Hey, where are you?

Jo: Your brother came over and is absolutely freaking out.

Jo: Your parents won't stop calling my house.

Jo: MJ is even texting me, it's weird.

Jo: Frankie. Come home. Please?

Nick: Frankie, you need to tell me where you are.

Nick: Please.

Nick: I'll come get you, I don't care.

Dad: Your mom is losing it, Frankie.

Dad: Please you have to come back. If not for her, do it for . . . I don't know, your brother, maybe?

Dad: I know you're mad at me, so not for me.

Dad: We love you. You have to know that.

Bella: What the hell Frankie, Jo says you ran away?!

Bella: What about the rally?

Bella: What about everything we're fighting for?!

Bella: You're just gonna bail when things get hard? You?! Of all people?

Bella: You told me to fight and now I'm in this mess all alone.

Bella: You're so disappointing.

Mom: Frankie. Please.

Chapter Nineteen

Frankie

At last, I've hit the ground running.

Is it cliché that I made a beeline straight to the East Village once I got off the bus? I feel like Miss Rishi has always tried to nudge us away from the cliché in our writing, but what if the cliché is what you're after? There's nothing wrong with craving something people claim they've seen too many times. If that were the case, Jo and I would have been called cliché for watching those *Paddington* movies several dozen times in junior high, at Preeti's sleepovers.

I thumb through a milk crate packed full of well-loved vinyl records on a table outside a record shop. Definitely don't have one of these in Greenport. Every album is under three dollars, though I don't recognize many of the bands and faces staring back at me. But that doesn't matter. This city is going to be full of things waiting for me to discover. I'm ready to uncover something new.

I flick back a few more records and spot a Sonic Youth album, *Murray Street*, with two kids on the cover playing under a net . . . and something twinges in my chest. Jo and I used to be like that, playing silly games and other nonsense before things moved the way they did as we got older. Less about playing in the sandbox and more about stealing kisses and holding hands in dark theaters. And she loves this band.

I want to buy it for her but . . . I'd have to go back.

And I don't even have that much money on me. Every penny is going to have to count. I also don't have a place to put the record. I guess I can fit it in my bag, but then what?

Standing here, outside this shop while people bustle by me, I suddenly feel like my backpack is a little heavier, my breath a little weightier. I look around, at this unfamiliar place with unfamiliar faces, and it hits me.

I don't have a plan.

Which is exciting and also wildly terrifying? Should I have thought this through more? Maybe I should have waited it out and left once Nick started at Harvard and crashed with him in Boston, but . . . I don't know what's going on with him. Would he have even let me? I don't know if I want anything to do with him right now. Or ever.

I slide the record back in and smile at the guy standing watch outside the shop, his tattooed arms crossed, a friendly grin on his pierced face. He nods at me and goes back to staring out at the street, and I'm so extremely jealous of whatever his life might be. Hanging out, keeping an eye on records, probably daydreaming about gigging with his punk band tonight.

I keep walking toward a patch of green and iron fencing down the block. Everyone at home keeps blowing up my phone, either with text messages or through social media, and it just keeps vibrating in my pocket. Everyone except Phoenix.

It keeps buzzing as Tompkins Square Park quickly comes fully into view, large, leafless elm trees stretching their bare winter limbs up into the New York City sky. A pack of puppies zips around inside a really large dog run, and I walk over to it, leaning against the fence. A few other people are there too, just dog watching, it seems, shooting videos on their phones or nudging each other to look at this dog or that.

Something twinges in my chest again, seeing a happy couple leaning against each other, here in this park.

I pull my phone out and swipe over to Phoenix. There's still no response since I messaged him on the bus here, to see if he was okay after fleeing my house. He looked fine, but still.

> **Me:** Hey, you get my texts?

A little blip, showing that he's typing, pops up on my screen, and it feels like my heart is going to flip over. He's there. He's seeing me.

> **Phoenix:** Texts? I don't think so. Sorry, my phone is being weird.

> **Me:** I'm in New York! Wandering the East Village, you should come!

Phoenix: New York? What's in New York?

Me: I ran away. My parents won't stop calling. I just can't deal with them anymore.

My mom calls again, and I swipe to ignore . . . and then just flip over to calling Phoenix.

"Oh, hey!" he says, but the phone sounds far away. "Hold on, Mom, just a second."

"Hey yourself." I smile, turning around, leaning against the dog park fence, the iron pressing against my back. Several skateboarders walk by, their boards under their arms, and I can see the skate park section of this place just a couple hundred feet away. There's so much life here. You can be fined for skateboarding in parks back home. Pretty sure if Mom and the neighborhood association had their way, you'd be charged for just *thinking* about it.

"I'm coming, Mom!" Phoenix says, still distant.

"Hey, you should come here!" I smile as though he can see it through the phone or something. "Take your mom's car, or grab the bus? There's a bus terminal not too far outside of Greenport. That's what I did."

"What?" Phoenix asks. "Wait, no. That . . . that sounds fun, but it's, like, a Tuesday, Frankie. I can't just bail on my family like that last minute."

Something about the way he says "bail" makes me wince. I didn't bail on mine; they've been slowly bailing on me.

"Come on," I plead. "We could . . . go to Central Park and sprawl out on the Great Lawn and look at the stars . . . I think Central Park is around here. Maybe?"

"It's not," someone says, walking by without stopping. Great. Thanks.

"Look, Frankie, I'm sorry but I have to go," Phoenix says, sounding more irritated than anything else.

"What?" I slide down to the sidewalk, sitting on the concrete. "Are you mad at me or something? What did I do?"

"No, please, of course I'm not mad at you," he says, and again, he sounds far away, like his phone is on the ground or a table. "It's just . . . things are a bit harried here at home and things got a little heavy last night. Jo was so pissed at us. Is she . . . Frankie, is she your girlfriend?"

"I don't want to talk about that."

"Yeah, but you said you weren't dating anyone, and that was . . . it was messed up. I jumped out a window and fell off a roof."

"I said I didn't have a boyfriend," I huff. "I didn't lie."

"Yeah, but you didn't tell the truth either. Hold on, Mom, I'll be right up." Suddenly his voice is close to the phone again. "Look, my sister is having a hard time with her feeding tube, I have to go."

"Feeding tube?"

"Yeah, she's sick, remember?" he says, sounding a little angrier at me now. "The whole reason we moved to your town? Things got abruptly worse today. I have to help take care of my family, they need me here, I can't just skip out."

"Oh . . . yeah, no, I remember." I wince. "I just . . . there's a lot going on here."

"Here too," he says, like I should know better.

"Well, okay, I'll let you go. I love you."

There's a pause.

And it's way too long.

"Phoenix? Are you going to say it?"

"I . . . Frankie, I can't. Not yet."

"What?!"

"It's just . . . that's big. That means a lot. It should be the right time and—"

"This can't be the right time?! I kind of need to hear it."

"Well, we're just so new," he says, sounding panicked. I can hear him swallow. "I don't know if we're there yet—"

"Right, so it was fun to hook up with someone new and different and exotic, but loving me is just impossible, right?"

"Frankie, you know I'm not like that. Come on, I—"

I hang up and cram the phone in my pocket.

It keeps buzzing. It could be Phoenix calling me back. Or maybe it's Dad or Mom, calling yet again in their frantic attempts to figure out where I am.

Goddamn it, Phoenix.

You're just like everyone else.

I should have known.

Phoenix: Hey where are you in New York?

Phoenix: Your brother figured out where I live and he's here all mad.

Phoenix: Frankie you have to talk to your family or like me or Jo.

Phoenix: Jo is even here! We're cool now!

Phoenix: Okay we're not she won't even look at me, but still.

Bella: So. Hi Nick.

Bella: You bail on me when I need you the most.

Bella: And so does your sister.

Bella: And you still won't answer any of my messages.

Bella: So fuck it, I'm coming over, and I'm not leaving until I get some answers.

Bella: I deserve answers.

Chapter Twenty

Bella

Whew.

I'm staring at the door to Nick's house. The Healy family. He hasn't been answering any of my messages or calls, seems to be ignoring me on social media . . . honestly, much like the rest of the school and everyone. It's been days of getting sent classroom and homework assignments from teachers, because God forbid I fall behind on anything while I'm in a grief spiral over what happened to me, to all my relationships, to my family, who went from being a wholesome cliché to being full of understandable rage. And once an hour or two of homework is finished, then it's seemingly endless marathons of Netflix shows and movies with Mom, who awkwardly googles every single program to check for potential triggers.

It's over the top, and . . . I love her so much.

And if there's one of many things I've learned during all this, it is that I deserve more. People who care about me at that level. Answers. Justice. A voice.

And while there's no way in hell I'm ready to, or even want to, talk to Andrew . . . Nick was there. One of my closest friends, a boy whom I cared about and who I thought cared for me. And I want to hear it from him, why he's been silent, when he should be screaming.

I exhale and walk toward the door.

You deserve more, you deserve more, you deserve—

I squint at the door. It's open a crack, and I knock before giving it a little nudge.

"Hello?" I venture, peeking inside the home. The living room is empty, and it's pretty quiet. I'm guessing someone left the door open in a hurry on the way out, which doesn't surprise me. The Healys are the kind of family that's well-off enough to not care about their home being broken into. I text Nick to let him know I'm at his house, but I don't expect an answer.

Why would he say anything, or do anything, now?

"Frankie?!" a frantic voice calls, startling me. Mrs. Healy peers out from the kitchen and hurries into the living room, and I open the door a little more. Her face completely drops at the sight of me. "Oh. Bella," she says, a bit breathless. "Hi."

"Hi, Mrs. Healy," I manage. "Can I talk to Nick?"

"Oh." She shakes her head and sniffles, balling a fist like she's trying to support herself. "No, no. He's not home right now."

"He hasn't been returning my texts or calls, and I kinda need to talk to him."

"I'm sorry," she says. "Can I help you? Is there something I can do?"

"No." I laugh a little. "It's a bit of a complicated situation, really."

"I know," Mrs. Healy says, deflating a bit. "I've heard about what happened—"

"Of course you did."

"I just . . ." she says, straining. "Do you want a glass of water? Soda? Something?"

"Oh, um . . ."

She walks back toward the kitchen, waving her hand for me to come in.

I glance around the living room, staring at the photos of the Healy family, all picture perfect. I feel like on any other day, I wouldn't hate seeing that so much. A week ago, I would have smiled along with Nick and Frankie, their joy-filled parents.

But now? My mom just cries around the house, and my dad keeps getting in screaming matches on the phone with lawyers and local media, who seem to think this is a story. Me and Andrew Montefiore. Like it's not something horribly traumatic and instead is some kind of small-town gossip infotainment. Like it isn't spiraling my entire life the way Andrew would spiral a goddamn football.

Mrs. Healy walks back into the living room, a Sprite in hand. She tosses me the can, and I tap on the top, waiting for whatever fizz is inside to calm down.

"Bella, I . . . want you to know that I understand how you feel right now," she says, taking a seat on the couch in the living room. She motions me over, but I stay standing, leaning against the wall. I pop open the soda with a loud *psssst* and take an immediate, too-long sip, the bubbles stinging my throat.

"I doubt that," I say, exhaling.

"I . . ." Mrs. Healy starts, wringing her hands. "Something similar happened to me once. Same story as yours, really. And after all of it, I was just . . . so angry. But mostly, I was angry at myself."

"Yourself?" I ask, talking barely above a whisper. I was not expecting this, when I came over. Mrs. Healy looks like she's about to crumble into dust, right here. She's trembling, looking down into her hands, which she keeps clenched together.

"I'd put myself in the situation, and . . . in a perfect world, these things wouldn't happen. But we have to be strong, accept our mistakes, and move on."

"Accept our . . . wait, move on?" I blink, trying to grasp what she just said: that I should just swallow my anger and shrug all this off. "When did it happen to you?"

"It's not important."

"If it's not important, you can say it."

"In college," she says quickly, like she has to get the words out before she chokes them back. "It feels like it was a million years ago, but it doesn't matter anymore. I moved on."

"When did you start to feel better?" I ask, and there's this flare of anxiety in my chest, dreading the answer.

Mrs. Healy stares down at her hands, and they stop shaking. Like she's freezing them with her eyes, willing all these feelings to go away.

"Mrs. Healy?" I press. "Tell me when I'm going to feel normal again."

Her hands start to quiver again, and she shakes her head, placing her face in her trembling hands.

Shit.

"Well, that's just great." I swallow, fighting the sob that's pushing its way up through my chest. "Thanks . . . thanks for the drink."

"Bella," Mrs. Healy says, looking up. There are tears streaking her cheeks. "You have to learn . . . we're all just magnets for predators."

"Well, this magnet for predators is learning."

I rush out of the house, hurrying to the sidewalk. I glance back and spot Nick's car in the driveaway. I look around for him for a second, wondering if I missed him coming in somehow, and shake my head.

Fuck it.

Fuck *him*.

What can he do?

I take my phone out of my pocket and start scrolling.

I know what *I* can do.

Bella: Hey all. Tomorrow there's going to be a rally downtown.

Bella: Right by the Montefiore statue near city hall.

Bella: And I'm fighting back.

Kelsey: Whoa there are a lot of people in this text chain.

Lily: Yeah. Hi. I don't know most of these numbers.

Kelsey: Well, this is me, Kelsey.

Emily: Em.

Julia: This is Julia Stone.

Lauren: Hi, Lauren here. And you better believe I'm in.

Kelsey: And I'm in.

Emily: Same.

Lily: Hell yeah.

Julia: Me too but aren't Frankie and Jo running something like this? We were working on posters just the other day. What happened?

Bella: I'm leading the charge now.

Bella: It's my story. It's my fight.

Bella: And I'm taking it all back.

Chapter Twenty-One

Nick

I walk in through the kitchen after parking my car in the driveway, just in time to see someone bolt out of the house.

"Mom?" I look around and spot her on the couch in the living room, where she's been sitting and sobbing since Frankie left the house. There are fresh tears on her cheeks, and her eyes are red. "What's going on?"

"Nothing," she says, shaking her head. "Your sister is still gone, but I'm gonna make her favorite quiche. She'll be home soon, and when she's home, she'll be hungry—"

"Who was that?" I ask, walking toward the front door. I peer outside, looking up and down the street, and duck back in. "The, um, this detective. He wants to talk to me."

"What?!" she snaps, getting up quickly from off the couch. "No, no, you have nothing to do with what happened to that girl."

"No, Mom, I have to tell you what happened at the party," I say. "I should have said something, I should have done something before, but it was like . . . between you pushing me to stay put and all this guilt, it's like . . . it's like I blocked it out or something."

"Nick—"

"I just . . . I remember Andrew saying that he was gonna make sure Bella was okay when I left. And now, I just can't stop thinking about Bella and that promise and the way he was looking at me . . ." I wince, and it almost feels like the memory is threatening to give me a headache. "I can see it. Andrew nudging Bella away from the rest of the party, trying to keep her close. How she tried to push him away but couldn't, and how maybe . . . I should have said something. Done something.

"But I was feeling . . . jealous? I thought maybe she wanted to be there, and that's the problem with all of this, isn't it? And I didn't do anything. I even . . . I even saw her in his room, sleeping. I should have stayed there, in that room, but he said he would take care of her and . . . goddamn it. Instead, I left and came home, and . . . I didn't keep her safe. I didn't protect her, and I should have been there while he kept handing out the drinks. I knew better and I did nothing. I just drank with my stupid friends and came home.

"Mom, Frankie was right about me. She's right about me."

"You saw all that," Mom says, walking toward me. "And you didn't do anything?"

"I don't think . . . I don't think I really knew what I was seeing when I was seeing it?" I venture. "If that makes sense? And then when he took her upstairs, and I saw her on his bed, he said . . . he said he'd take care of her. He promised. He looked at me and he *promised*."

"Nick—"

"She was unconscious, and I walked away. I didn't do anything. What if . . . what if that had been Frankie?"

My mom just stands there, looking at me.

"Mom, just tell me what to do!" I shout. I'm breathing heavy; my heart is racing. My throat is dry and I'm shaking. "Just tell me what to do, please!"

She exhales and looks down at her hands before speaking. She always has all the answers. What classes to take, what clubs to join, what friends to spend my time with. Which homework assignments to work on over others. She's helped manage every single piece of my life up until now, and while I've had so much resentment bubbling around that fact, now I just want that comfort again. *Just . . . fix everything, Mom. Please.*

"You can't repeat this to anyone," she says, her voice gone cold.

"But people think Bella is lying! They're going to think Frankie is making it up, that Jo is making it up. I'm . . . I'm the only witness."

"If you have to talk to the police, you tell them you were at the party and you left. You didn't see anything."

"What?" I scoff. "No. That's . . . Mom, I just told you that I saw everything."

"Did you, though? You think you saw the start of something. If something like this goes public, it'll follow you for the rest of your life. What about your admission to Harvard? They could take it away. They do that sort of thing, you know. I've read about it happening."

"Why would someone punish me for telling the truth?"

"They wouldn't. They'd punish you for drinking, maybe call you an accomplice for leaving Bella there with him."

"No, no, that can't be right." I shake my head; this isn't what I need. This isn't what I wanted to hear. "You're . . . you're just mad at me for not doing something in the moment, and now that I want to make it right, you're telling me not to. What about Bella?"

"You can't help her now. You can't undo what happened. You'll just ruin your life."

"My life." I nod and suck at my teeth. "Is that what this is about? Or is it about *your* life. That's what you're scared of, isn't it? It's not about me, it's about what your friends and these neighborhood people are going to say."

"Nick, we have worked too hard for this to lose it all overnight." She takes a step forward, pointing at me. "We earned this."

"No." I shake my head. "No, I messed up, Mom. If I lose everything, I deserve it."

I storm out of the house.

It might be too late to chase down Bella.

But I can chase the truth.

Frankie: Jo.

Frankie: Please.

Frankie: I messed up, and now I'm stuck here, and you're the only one I can talk to.

Frankie: Can you come get me?

Frankie: Please?

Jo: Come get you.

Jo: In New York City.

Frankie: It's . . . not that far?

Jo: Fuck, Frankie!

Jo: That's so unfair. You know I can't say no.

Frankie: Sure you can.

Jo: No. I can't.

Jo: Drop a pin and send me a link to wherever you are.

Frankie: Thank you.

Jo: Don't.

Chapter Twenty-Two

Frankie is sitting on a bench, looking cold.

Which isn't terribly surprising. It's New York City. It's nighttime. It's winter and she's got on that leather jacket, a T-shirt, and stupid shorts. I can't help but shake my head as I walk toward her, so angry at how selfish and stupid she's been. It's the first time I've ever been disappointed by her clothing choices, and for a second, I think of her ridiculous mother. Her mom who is back at home, having meltdowns over all of this. Her mom who was right about this one thing, I suppose.

She looks up from the bench and does a double take when she sees me.

"Oh my God," she says, getting up and running over to me. "Thanks for coming, I . . . I didn't have enough money for the train home, and then my debit card wasn't working, and I didn't want to call Mom or Dad, and . . . where's Dottie the Datsun?"

She smiles at me, a dimple cratering her cheek, like

everything is just . . . okay. Like she can reference my disaster of a car and wipe away the last day of heartbreak.

It's not okay.

It's never going to be okay again.

"I'm parked around the corner," I say, nodding behind me. I turn around and make my way down the street. New York City. Parking was hell on Earth, and if my car is still there, I will be utterly amazed. The parking sign had parking signs, and I'm pretty sure the meter had a ticket on it for daring to be there too long.

"Awesome," she says, walking after me. "That was, um, pretty crazy, back at my house?"

I don't turn around. I don't say anything.

"I'm surprised you showed up," she says.

"I'm your best friend," I say through gritted teeth, even though that doesn't feel entirely true right now. "I'm not going to leave you stranded in a neighborhood you can't even name."

"I'm in the East Village!" she exclaims proudly.

"No, you're not." I reel around. "Maybe you were before, but you see that?" I point at the huge white arch looming over a nearby park, bright white against the dark. "That's the Washington Square Arch. You made it about a mile from the East Village before you called me."

"No . . ." Her face scrunches up. "No way, I was exploring and walking around for a while!"

"In a circle maybe," I scoff, and keep walking, looking for my car.

"You're mad."

"Oh!" I laugh. "Can you guess why?"

"I'm sorry. I am," she says, hurrying to walk next to me. "I was going to tell you and—"

"And yet you didn't." I stop walking and glare at her. "Because you knew what you were doing was wrong, playing us both like that."

"I didn't think I was going to fall that hard for him, you know?" She looks down at her shoes and back up at me. "I just, I fell in love with him."

"Of course you did." I keep walking. "Congrats. I'm glad you found something healthy and rational. I'm clearly not as legit as your fuckboy Phoenix."

"It's not like that," she says. "I didn't think we were in a serious, like, real relationship, you know? You and me."

I stop walking again and have to take a few breaths. I know she didn't mean to end that statement with "you and me," our go-to sign of affection, but there it is. Like a dagger in the back.

"Right." I grit my teeth. "Because why would you take this seriously. Take *me* seriously."

"You know I didn't mean it like that—"

"I thought you were . . . I thought you could have been the one person who saw me. Who really saw me."

"I do! I am! I—"

"Listen," I snarl through my teeth. "I want you to know that, even though you've hurt me? I'm happy for you. All right? You and Phoenix. I want nothing but the best, because you're my best friend, regardless of how you've just . . . cast me aside like that. But for someone who is always so terrified and so worried about being that throwaway person to other people, to your family, it's pretty fucking brutal. You talk about how you feel left behind and ignored, forgotten about at family events and by your brother. But the second someone new and shiny came along, the *second*, you did to me what you fear the most."

"Jo—"

"You abandoned me. And you abandoned your friends, the people counting on you. Bella's trying to plan the rally all on her own now, you know that? I've been getting texts from people the last twenty-four hours, wondering where you are. Your family, people at school."

I ball my fists, trying not to cry. I'm not gonna let her see me cry. I practiced everything I wanted to say enough in the car, teared up enough in the car, tried to use them before I saw her.

"And with my family, *my family*, treating me the way they do . . . it's a walk in the park for you, you know that?" I shake my head. "Does he know . . . does Phoenix know how you told me you'd love me until you died?"

"I—"

"*Because you're still alive*, Frankie! How isn't that a serious relationship?!" I snap, turning away and walking a few feet before turning back. "And another thing—"

She's standing still, looking at her phone. I charge over.

"What the fuck?!" I yell, nearly slapping her phone out

243

of her hand. "Is it him? Now? You'd talk to him right now in the middle of—"

"No, no, Jo," she says, trembling.

"Do you think I give a shit what he has to—"

"No!" she screams. "It's not him, it's . . . it's my mom. Something's wrong. We have to go!"

Dad: Frankie I know how mad you are at us.

Dad: But you need to come home right now.

Dad: Your mother is in the hospital and she isn't waking up.

Nick: Where are you.

Nick: Something happened, you need to answer your phone.

Nick: Or just answer these texts.

Nick: Did Jo find you yet?

Chapter Twenty-Three

I can't remember the last time I was in a hospital. The plastic of the chairs in the waiting room feels weirdly like the seats in the bus and the train station downtown and makes me feel like I'm just . . . sitting here, killing time until I head off somewhere new.

Like . . . this is the start of something, in a place where things often end.

Mom.

Damn.

How didn't I see it?

Dad paces around in front of me, his feet making a rhythmic snap against the hard white floor, almost like a clock that's ticking at half the speed but shows no sign of slowing down. He keeps rubbing his face with his hands, as though he can wipe away what he saw. What we both saw.

Mom, on the floor in the living room, pills spilled all over the ground.

Not moving.

A doctor walks through the waiting room doors, and all the eyes of every other person in here seem to look up at him. I see their heads rise, their bodies shift. Like this man carries all their hopes and answers. And in a lot of ways, I suppose he does.

"Healy?" he asks, and Dad just bolts over to him.

"Are you Dr. Woodson?" Dad asks, as I get up and walk over to join him. Dad immediately wraps his arm around me, like he's bracing me for something awful, but it feels more like I'm the one holding him up.

"Yes, you're, um, Steve?" he asks, and then holds up a clipboard, looking at some papers before his eyes flit back to us.

"Yeah, yeah." My dad nods, his tone eager. "Can you give us any updates? How is MJ? Ah—Mary Jane?"

"Well, it's . . ." The doctor looks at me and back to my dad. "Would you rather talk about this in private?"

"No, it's okay," Dad insists. "This is my son, Nick, he saw . . . everything."

"I understand, it's just . . ." The doctor sighs.

"Please," Dad says. "He can handle it."

"Okay." The doctor nods. "Well, in addition to the oxycodone, we found fentanyl in her system."

"Wait, what?" Dad gasps, and lets go of me, stepping toward the doctor. "That's . . . no, that isn't possible." He tries to peek at the clipboard and the doctor shifts away from him. "Please, what's going on?"

"Mr. Healy. Nick." Dr. Woodson exhales. "Oxycodone is

often contaminated with fentanyl. It can happen if she got counterfeit pills off the street."

"No." Dad shakes his head. "No, she . . . had a prescription. She got in a car accident in the summer and was still having trouble with her back. I've seen the bottles, and look, I know sometimes she would maybe take one or two extra, and there was the wine . . . Oh God." My dad has his hands on his face again. "I just . . . I thought it was fine, she had a prescription."

"Actually, um . . ." The doctor looks at me again, wincing, and I can tell he still isn't sure how much of this I should be hearing. And honestly, I'm not sure how much I should be hearing either. "Your wife doesn't have a current prescription. Not with any of the doctors you wrote down."

"This has to be a mistake." Dad looks out at the waiting room. I can hear that same shifting noise again, and everyone is looking away this time, which means they were staring at the scene unfolding. "She's an amazing mother. She is. She's obsessed with her health, makes these . . . these gross Paleo meals. Does she look like a drug addict to you?"

"What do you think a drug addict looks like, Mr. Healy?" Dr. Woodson asks, and wow, if that doesn't feel wildly uncomfortable.

"I'm sorry, I'm sorry," Dad mutters, looking down.

"Doctor, is she going to be okay?" I ask, stepping up.

"Um . . . well, we have a lot to discuss," he says, which isn't a yes or a no, and I'm not sure how to take that.

"Nick, could you go wait for Frankie?" Dad asks, barely looking up at me.

I sigh and nod, and he pats me on the shoulder, holding on to me for a minute with a firm, loving shake, before I walk over to the waiting area again. But instead of taking our old seats, I gather our jackets and move closer to where Dad and the doctor are. Or, at least, the closest I can get.

No prescription.

I think about the last week or so. That heated argument on the phone that wasn't with Dad but with someone else. The blur of a person rushing away from our house. The pills and the wine on the countertop. The way she's been sweating and teetering like she's about to fall apart. All the signs—all of them—were right there.

I squint as though that'll help me hear better and lean back into my chair, the two of them not too far behind me.

"There could be serious long-term consequences with an overdose like this, Mr. Healy. I just need to be honest with you there." Dad mumbles something in response to the doctor, and he keeps going. "We have her on buprenorphine to help with the withdrawal symptoms, which are going to be pretty severe, but once she's discharged, I really recommend inpatient recovery."

"Okay, okay," Dad says, clearing his throat.

"I'll be back in a few minutes, and then you and the family can come back and see her," Dr. Woodson says. "She might still be out, but I think she'll be awake any minute now."

"Thank you, Doctor. Truly," Dad says, and I glance over just in time to catch Dad walking toward me. He stops by where our seats were and turns to see me. He smirks and shakes his head.

"You think you're just so smart, don't you?" He sits and tussles my hair. "How much of that did you hear?"

"Besides the part where Mom might have to go into a facility? Not much."

"Listen, Nick, I know it's—"

The doors to the waiting room swing open, on the opposite side this time, and Frankie barrels in. She makes eye contact with me and Dad, her eyes wide, frantic, and runs over to us.

"This is my fault," she says, collapsing into my arms, and I hug her tight.

"It's not, it's not," I say, rubbing her back.

"Dad, I'm sorry." She lets go of me, and Dad's face breaks as he hugs her. "I was so angry and feeling alone and just . . ."

"Don't worry about it, sweetheart," Dad says, letting her go. "It's not important. We'll all get through it, we will."

"Mr. Healy?" Dr. Woodson is back and waves us over. He looks at Frankie, a bit confused for a second.

"My daughter," Dad says. "Frankie, this is Dr. Woodson."

"We're taking good care of . . ." The doctor glances at Dad and back at Frankie. "Good care of your mother."

Dad nods, and I can't help but smirk. The doctor risked it all instead of saying "stepmother" or something and got it right. Good for him.

"Good," Frankie says, crossing her arms. I half expect

her to let him have it for that moment of hesitation, but she just looks at me and shrugs. It feels . . . almost like a splash of normalcy again, like we're at the breakfast table busting each other's chops. I wonder if we'll get there again.

"All right, follow me."

Dr. Woodson leads us through the waiting room doors and down a hallway. Everything is lit by the same harsh fluorescent lights I assume are in every single hospital ever, because it's absolutely what you see on television and in movies. The floors and walls are immaculate, and save for the shuffling of feet and the sound of rolling carts, it's almost silent here. We pass a few patient rooms, and I can make out some feet standing inside, bodies all blocked by large paper-fabric curtains, so there are people here.

It's just . . . they're all so quiet.

Like Mom. On that floor in our living room. Silent, barely breathing, lolling back in Dad's arms like a child's rag doll, while I frantically called an ambulance.

This is going to be one of those things that I carry with me forever, like a snapshot staple-gunned to my brain.

Dr. Woodson slows down and stops at a room.

"Here we are," he says, and we all move to walk inside when he stops us. "I, um, just want to prepare you. It can be really jarring to see a loved one hooked up to all these machines and tubes, but know that we're doing everything we can to help her recover. And what you're going to see might look scary, but it's not."

Frankie looks at me and rolls her eyes.

I can't help but smirk. Even now, after all this, she's still my snarky disaster of a sister.

"And when you're ready, here." The doctor hands my dad a little pamphlet with a lovely building on the front, all big, bold glass windows, and sprawling green lawns. "Deptford Recovery Center" in a friendly font on the paper. Dad opens it up and looks through it, nodding.

"Thank you, Doctor," my dad says, and gives Frankie a little nudge with his elbow. "We appreciate it."

Dad steps inside. Frankie and I follow, and every step feels like one step closer to some kind of new future. Like, this changes things. Nothing is going to be the same after this. And I'm not sure what barreled us forward here to this moment, all of us together in Mom's hospital room while she recovers from a near fatal overdose, but I think it was a little bit of all of us.

Me, trying so hard to keep an eye on everyone and be perfect, that I missed everything and messed things up.

Frankie, wanting so badly to be seen and loved, that she tried to push away the people who see and love her.

And Dad, for all his time away and trying to bring Mom closer, which only pushed her the same distance that he'd been pushing himself.

It's that car crash. That was the moment that flung us here. She was alone in the car, so none of us really know what it was like for her. Bad enough that she needed pain meds, but not bad enough that she needed them for that long.

The accident is still happening, only the twisted metal

and burning rubber is my family, misshapen and broken in ways that maybe aren't repairable.

Mom stirs a little in the bed, as Dad caresses her hand, his eyes closed. He's whispering something, maybe a prayer, I don't know, when she wakes up. She blinks her eyes a bunch, but they are just so impossibly red, I'm not sure how she can even see through them. And maybe she can't, because she closes them again, before smacking her lips together and breathing deeply.

"Are you . . . embarrassed?" she asks.

"Damn it, MJ, no," Dad says, near tears. He inches closer to the bed. "Just embarrassed that I wasn't paying attention."

"Even if you were, I don't know if you would have noticed." She coughs a little and swallows, clearly having a hard time. She points at something off to the side, and I notice some water across the room. I fill a cup for her, and Frankie takes it from me, her eyes pleading with me to have this moment. We don't even need to say anything to each other.

Frankie walks over and hands Mom the cup, but Mom reaches out, brushing Frankie's hand.

"Frankie," she says, still not opening her eyes. "I'm . . . I'm sorry . . ."

"No, I'm sorry, Mom."

"I'm good at hiding things," Mom says. "Me and your father, we've been married twenty years and he still doesn't know shit about me." She laughs a little and then coughs, and my dad just shakes his head. "But you . . . you've been hiding so much." She forces her eyes open, squinting at Frankie, and reaches her shaking hand out. Frankie bends down, and Mom cups her cheek with her hand. "I'm sorry. If you were hiding, I should have been seeking. I'm your mom. It's my job."

Frankie lets out a little sob and leans onto Mom's shoulder in the hospital bed. Mom winces at something, and Frankie pulls away.

"It's okay," Mom says, gritting her teeth and gesturing at herself. "It all hurts." She looks at my dad, her eyes widening a little more. "Steve, I need help."

"Well, you're about to get three months of it, I think," Dad says, smiling a little, though he's definitely crying. He holds up the pamphlet the doctor gave him. "There's an inpatient program here, in a nearby building. The kids can visit on the weekend. There's even a therapy dog named Augustus."

"Wow," Mom says, sarcasm oozing from her scratchy voice. "I cannot wait."

"Maybe . . ." Dad looks at me and Frankie, like he's unsure about what he's going to say. "Maybe we can help each other too. Like the therapist said. I never wanted you to think work was more important than you, than the kids." He looks at Frankie. "I know—I know I messed up pushing you away, and I missed a lot. I'm sorry, all of you. I'm a mess."

"I'm detoxing from opiates, Steve. I win."

Frankie snorts out a laugh and leans against me. I give her a side hug.

"Nick, Frankie, come here," Mom says, waving me over. "I'm . . . I was wrong. Forget what people think of us. You have to go to the police. You have to do the right thing, tell them everything. I, um . . ." She looks at Dad and swallows roughly. "I told Bella what I went through, just like her, in college."

"MJ." Dad winces.

"Mom—" Frankie starts.

"It's okay." Mom rushes the words out, shaking her head a little. "We can talk more about it later. Nick, have you . . . have you talked to Bella?"

"Mom," I say with a small sigh, "I don't think I can face her."

"You have to," Mom says. "You can't walk away from this."

I look over at Frankie, who nods her head. "I'll go with you."

Kelsey: Hey, where is everyone meeting?

Kelsey: I was planning to just plant myself down by the statue, but I don't want to be the only one there if you're all meeting somewhere else.

Lily: Good question. Thoughts?

Julia: I can do the statue.

Lauren: I'm hitting the café before the rally, anyone want anything?

Lauren: It's pretty damn cold out, so a little something warm is probably a good call.

Lily: Why didn't we hang out more this year? You're a genius.

Lauren: I try, I try.

Kelsey: Bella? You there?

Kelsey: If you're having a hard time, we can come meet you at your house?

Kelsey: We're all here for you.

Frankie: Hey.

Frankie: I know you probably don't want to hear from me, or anyone in my family, for that matter.

Frankie: But I'm back, and I'm showing up today.

Nick: Hey. I'd love it if we could talk before the rally. Or after.

Nick: I know I've got a lot to apologize for.

Chapter Twenty-Four

Frankie

I can't remember the last time the house was so quiet.

There have been plenty of awkward silences here, maybe too many. Pauses that felt like they were pregnant with all the words no one wanted to say but desperately needed to. And I can see those words now, unspoken and painful between these walls.

Mom's suffering with her pain medication and drinking, Dad wrestling with his need for affection while pushing everyone away, Nick being crushed under the weight of all this pressure from, well, everyone.

Me feeling like I don't belong in my own family.

But instead of sitting down and just talking about it, all of us let those feelings fester until the wound nearly killed us. And not in some metaphorical way, but literally. Mom's still in the hospital. Nick . . . let Andrew rape somebody.

I lean forward on the couch, the same couch I've spent so many stolen moments with Jo on, kissing and snuggling under the ancient, vintage comforters my mom swears are beautiful but feel like sandpaper. A bit of a too on-the-nose image for me. I'm that comforter, at least for Jo, and I wish I knew how to fix what I've broken there.

But I don't think there is a way to do that. And I think . . . I think I have to find a way to be okay with that.

"Listen, I don't care how much it costs, I want it booked," Dad snaps in the kitchen, startling me a little. I almost spill the coffee I forgot I was holding. "Our insurance can figure it all out later."

I feel like he's been on the phone since we got home last night, just nonstop back and forth with this inpatient place, his job, some insurance company . . . a lot of stuff I honestly don't quite understand, and I'm afraid to.

I wonder if this is what Phoenix and his family deal with, with his sister. How much does he take on? I feel like I never really asked him much, not in the way I should have. Here I am, being another scratchy comforter for someone who seemed to really start caring about me.

I guess the best I can do is focus on what I can control right now, and Bella's rally is happening. I can show up for her.

I get up off the couch and head upstairs, catching a look from Dad, who is still on the phone, madly writing something down. He offers up a quick smile that I know is forced. I'm not sure how he's holding anything together. It's also weird to see him home, right now, at this time of day.

"Hm?" he says into his phone. "No, I'm not coming in today, James. And if that's a problem, you can all just fuck off! Hello? Yes, sorry—"

Well.

I guess he's changed a little bit.

I peek at Nick's door on my way to my room. It's closed, and I hear the soft hum of some music from inside. I step over and ball my fist up to knock, but stop and turn away. He's got a lot to process right now, and I'm not sure anything I could say will make things better.

And maybe that's the problem.

I don't know.

Always wondering what action will fix things, when really, all I think is that the people around me want to be heard. Just like me. I wonder what it is that Nick has to say right now and when he'll be ready to say any of it. Mom wants him to talk to Bella, but God, I cannot imagine how that will go.

This is all a lot.

And my bedroom basically twists my heart up in a knot. My bed, it's still . . . rumpled. From me and Phoenix. And right near it is a pile of poster supplies from Jo and my protests. Just . . . there. Like witnesses.

I shake my head.

I need to get through this and make my apologies later.

I wrangle up the paper and pens and markers, tossing whatever will fit into a tote bag, and move to head downstairs. I stop at the edge of the first step, then walk over to Nick's room, and this time I don't hesitate. I knock.

"Hey," I say, and lean my head against his door. The music stops, but I don't hear any movement or his voice. "Just . . . I'm going to work on some of the posters downstairs if you want to help. Might be fun?"

I listen for a beat, but I don't hear anything. The music is still off, though.

"All right, I'll be in the living room," I say, pressing my hand to the door. I turn away and make my way downstairs and hear the doorbell chime. I hurry down into the living room and swing the door open.

"Frankie!" exclaims Mrs. Howell, one of Mom's friends and one of the women on the PTA board with her. Mrs. Hoffman is right behind her, along with Mrs. Bailey. I don't know their kids too well—Jennifer, Rich, and . . . I'm not sure who Mrs. Bailey's kid is. I know she does the PTA too, but I think her son graduated, like, two years ago? I don't get parents who stay involved like that with their schools when their kids are long gone.

"Hey, Mrs. Howell," I say, glancing back at Dad. He peers into the living room from the kitchen, his phone still in his hand, and he's noticeably scowling. "What do you—"

"We just wanted to check on MJ," Mrs. Howell says, and the other two women behind her nod, almost solemnly.

"I wish we would have known she was an . . . addict," Mrs. Bailey says, wincing. Mrs. Howell puts a hand on her shoulder, like the weight of this discussion is going to knock her over. "We would have tried to do something. Be there for her, organize a fundraiser, you know?"

"No one should go through that alone," Mrs. Howell says.

"She's not alone. She has us. Me, my dad—"

"Well, Frankie." Mrs. Howell's expression softens. "We both know just how involved Steve—"

"Hey!"

Dad thunders into the living room, gesturing at the ladies with his phone.

"My wife dealt with your special brand of poison for years. *Years*." I have never seen him this worked up. Even when he and Mom would bicker and fight, he never turned another color like this. His neck and cheeks are flushing red, like he's just been out on a run, not just walking quickly across the house. "Get the hell out and stay away from my kid."

"Wow, Steve," Mrs. Howell snorts. "We just came over to see if there was anything we could do and—"

"And get some gossip to spread around your friends," Dad snaps back. "You know, I know pieces of this are my fault. I know it, and I own it. But you? Your whole bunch? She spent all this time trying to desperately live up to your approval. And why? Who are you? What have you done? Why are you so important?"

"Steve—" Mrs. Howell tries to interject, taking a step into the house.

"No." He points at her foot and the door. "Out. I don't want you taking literally a single step in here. MJ deserved so much better than you all these years. Better than me. And I'm going to make sure she has it. Starting right now."

He takes another step toward the women, who back off down the little set of stairs outside our front door.

And with that, he slams the door and heads back into the kitchen. Like nothing happened. Like he was just checking the mail and not erupting at Mom's circle of friends.

I . . . like this new Dad.

I peer out the front door's little glass windows, standing on my tiptoes to get a good look, and see the women already making their way down the sidewalk. They're all on their phones, barely watching where they are walking, and I wonder what they are saying. Who they are talking to. Who they are dishing our family's business . . .

Hm.

"Dad?" I venture, walking into the kitchen. He glances over at me, and he's got a paper towel in his hand, dabbing at his forehead. I can't help the smile that cracks my face, and he shakes his head at me.

"Don't." He points, laughing a little through his nose. "That took a lot out of me."

"It was awesome," I say. "I'm proud of you."

There's a quiet beat in the kitchen, hold music on his phone filling the silence.

"Dad, how . . . how did they know about Mom already?" I ask.

"Hard to say." He shrugs. "It's this town, Frankie. Gossip travels fast. Maybe a nurse said something to someone at home, or one of the doctors. Unless . . . your mother . . ."

He glances at his phone and then looks at me.

"Can I see your phone?" he asks.

"Dad!" I exclaim, placing my hand on my pocket, my phone tucked away inside.

"Not to spy or anything . . . just . . ." He sticks his hand out, waving me over. "Just really quick. Go load up your mom's Instagram."

I slide my phone out and swipe over to Instagram, loading up her profile. It's just square after square of things in the house, whatever she's been cooking, all very cute and homemaker-ish, which is one of the many reasons I never really see her in my feed. I honestly have my mother on mute and that . . . makes me feel not so great now.

Especially when I see the newest post.

It's not some artfully arranged plate or a piece of reclaimed furniture or glassware. It's a square full of words.

Well. You're all going to hear it from someone eventually. So, it might as well be me. I'm in the hospital. Urgent care. My painkillers, which I shouldn't have been taking anymore, had fentanyl in them and I almost overdosed and died. My son found me. I'm off to get some help, something I should have asked for a long time ago but didn't really know I could. If you're also struggling, I hope you'll reach out to someone close to you. Before it's too late. It was almost too late for me.

There's a little "1/2" at the bottom, and when I swipe, there's a photo of Mom in her hospital bed, smiling a little at the camera, but her eyes are wet with tears. Like she just finished writing that bit of text, knowing fully well that "friends" like the ones who just came by were going to react exactly the way they did.

Fuck, Mom.

"Fuck, MJ."

I look up at Dad, and he's swiping at his eyes. He walks over into the dining room and practically collapses on a chair.

"Dad . . ." I say softly.

"It's okay." He sniffles loudly. "I just . . . How did we get here? I mean, I know the answer to that. I do. But Jesus."

"Hello?" his phone says in his hand.

"Oh!" Dad wipes at his face with his sleeve. "Hi, yes, hello. I'm calling about Mary Jane Healy? She . . ."

And he disappears into the kitchen and out into the yard. I can see him from the dining room table, through the window, animatedly talking. I take a seat back in the living room, on the couch, and start to spread out my poster boards, plucking out markers, pencils, some stencils, when Nick's footsteps catch my attention.

He doesn't take his usual playful jump and can barely look at me. His eyes flit up and back down toward the floor, as he makes his way over to the couch, sitting far on the other side.

"Can I help?" he asks, his voice breaking a little.

I glance up at him, and he finally manages to look at me. His face looks like porcelain, like it might crack apart at any minute.

I slide a poster board over to him and roll a few markers across the table.

Frankie: Hey.

Frankie: I don't know if you saw mom's post, but . . . things aren't great over here.

Frankie: Or maybe it's getting better, I'm not sure.

Frankie: I just want you to know I'm sorry.

Frankie: I feel like things went to hell here, at home, because no one would talk.

Frankie: And I just don't want that to be us, you know?

Jo: I saw it.

Jo: I appreciate this but . . . it already is us. You know that, right?

Jo: I'll be ready to talk eventually. You're my best friend.

Jo: But I'll need a minute.

Frankie: I know. I just had to say it.

Jo: I know.

Frankie: Hey. So. That phone call and the other night.

Frankie: That sure was something, right?

Phoenix: Well, yeah.

Phoenix: I'm sorry I couldn't give you what you needed, Frankie.

Phoenix: On the phone and . . . well, whatever this is. Was. I don't know.

Phoenix: I hope we can be cool. You're the coolest person I've ever met.

Phoenix: Also, maybe my only friend here?

Phoenix: Is that pathetic?

Frankie: No. No, absolutely not.

Frankie: And don't apologize, please.

Frankie: Maybe we can hit reset on this friendship in the new year, after the break?

Phoenix: I'd really like that.

Phoenix: You're really awesome, Frankie Healy.
Don't forget it.

Frankie: Not sure I believe you.

Frankie: But I'll try.

Chapter Twenty-Five

Phoenix

"What is that?" I ask, squinting at . . . well, I'm not quite sure. A bundle of string and a circular piece of fabric in what looks like a wooden frame. There's an array of colors on my sister's lap in the hospital bed, splashes of life on her stark white bedsheet. All these bits of string.

"I'm doing needlepoint." Her eyes flit up to me and back down, focusing intently on the circle in her hand. I can't help the laugh that erupts from my chest. She drops the needlework and glares at me. "Shut up."

"It's fine, I just didn't realize you suddenly became an old lady." I grab one of the chairs in the room and drag it across the floor, sitting down next to her.

"I'll have you know a lot of my friends back home do this." She shakes the needlepoint frame around, some of the string flapping about. I look at the board, and she flips it over so I can see the front of it, the back just a mess of color.

It just says I'LL REMAIN on it.

"What does that—" I start.

"It's from that Neil P. Bardhan novella you got me, *The Poker Player*. He's a favorite of Mom's too, you know. 'Whether you're cashing in or cashing out, something remains of you on the table.' Turns out it's kind of impossible to needlework that into something that's, like, a three-by-three-inch square." Ruby sighs at this, and it sounds like there's a sob caught in her throat somewhere.

I don't really get it. "That's . . . that's really lovely. But why that?"

"It's not really about poker."

She looks right at me.

"You know, we don't talk a lot about me being sick," Ruby says matter-of-factly. "Stuck here in this bed all these months. Well, this bed and the bed back at home."

Ruby inches herself back in the bed, sitting up a little bit more. A roll of string bounces off her leg, and I catch it before it can unspool all over the floor.

"Thanks. But . . . that quote, those books you get me all the time. About these close-knit families and all . . . I keep holding all of those stories close. Because staying here, for you and Mom, that fight is easier than the idea of letting go."

She hands me the needlepoint.

"I'm staying. I'm going to remain here." Ruby presses it into my hands and immediately grabs at her string and another one of those needlepoint frames. "I'm gonna make one for Mom too."

I clutch the little piece of art.

It looks so terrible.

And I love it.

I lean back in the hospital chair, rocking a little, and pull out my phone while Ruby does her needlework. She sucks through her teeth a few times, swiping at her finger, from pinpricks I'm guessing, as I swipe around on my phone.

It looks like Frankie is busy prepping for the rally. There's a bunch of photos on her Instagram of posters she's been working on, pictures of her various supplies: markers, glitter, chalk pens—the kind of stuff you'd maybe expect to see at an arts and crafts table, not being used to stir a revolution. But that's just Frankie, I've learned. Unexpected. A force.

And while I know whatever was happening with us is basically over, a fire that burned way too fast, way too soon, I think we'll find our way back to being friends. I'd really love that.

"You know," Ruby says, looking down at her needlework. "If you need to talk about it, about me and everything, you can." She glances up at me, a little smile on her face. "I'm not precious about this. And I know it's gotta be hard on you, us moving all the way here for me."

"It's fine."

She gives me a look.

"It really is. I'm making . . . friends?"

Her brow furrows at the question mark on the end of that statement, and I laugh.

And I update her on everything: Frankie and the date

around town and then . . . well, I leave out some details of my visit to her house. But she puts it together pretty easily and laughs at me. Then I tell her about Jo, about Frankie running away to New York and telling me she loved me, and now she's back for the rally for Bella.

"It's been . . . intense." I rub the back of my head. The needlework is sitting in her lap, abandoned, as she stares at me. "And now, I just don't know what to do next. I feel like I found and lost my people as quickly as they came, and—"

"Go get some art supplies," Ruby says.

"What?" I look in her lap and on the side table by her hospital bed. "Are you out of string? I don't understand—"

"No, you beautiful idiot." Ruby laughs. "I want to make a sign for that rally with you. And then you're going."

"Whoa, what? No way. I don't think they're going to want me there."

"Of course they want you there." She swipes at me, like she's trying to push me out of the room from where she's sitting. "There's a pharmacy around the corner from here. Just get some poster board and markers or something. It'll be a lot more fun than me making another one of these depressing signs for Mom and you doomscrolling over there."

"I wasn't doomscrolling."

She gives me a look.

"Okay, fine!" I get up and head out of her room, her laughter following me into the hallway.

· · ·

I'm pulling out a large piece of poster board from the back of this pharmacy, art and school supplies sitting right next to really crappy candles that look like the kind of gift you give someone you don't actually care much about, when my phone buzzes. I nab a few more sheets and a set of different-colored Sharpie markers and give the screen a look.

It's Frankie.

My heart slams in my chest.

I know we texted already and talked. I know this isn't a thing, but . . . that doesn't make it feel like any less of a thing still. The stupid heart wants what it wants. Maybe Ruby can embroider that on something for me to hang in my future college dorm room, right next to a LIVE, LAUGH, LOVE sign. Ugh.

I hate this.

But I know if Saundra were here, or Nwayieze, or anyone else from my little group back at home, they would tell me this'll make a good short story or a poem someday.

> **Frankie:** Hey.

There's a photo attached: she's waving a peace sign and there is a huge pile of poster boards on the couch in her living room. I can't really make out what's on them, they're a bit out of focus, but I can tell they are all marked up and ready to go.

274

> **Frankie:** The rally is today. And I know things are weird.

> **Frankie:** But it would mean a lot if you came.

> **Frankie:** Not just for me, but for Bella, you know?

I smile and clutch the art supplies tighter, thinking of my sister up in that hospital bed. This is the kind of thing she would have loved to go to. Even now, from her bed and swimming in treatments, she still finds the time to jump into hashtags on social media, spouting messages of support and resistance.

If she can do that under treatment . . .

. . . I can do this with a slightly broken heart.

> **Me:** I'll be there.

I hurry to the register.
There's work to be done.

Chapter Twenty-Six

As I walk into the town square, past the shops and boutiques and cafés I've spent so much of my life in with
Frankie, I keep reminding myself that this isn't about
her. Or me, really. I'm here for Bella. I recognize a number of kids from school, milling about, sitting on sidewalks with coffee cups and on benches in the square on
their phones.

It's a solid turnout. I'm pleasantly surprised.

I sit down on a curb and pull out my phone—

"Hey, Fabrics."

I drop it, the phone clattering onto the asphalt in front
of me. Kelsey scoops it up, her bright yellow nail polish
popping against the black street pavement. She hands
it to me, and I meet her eyes, a little smirk curving her
mouth up.

"He-hey, Kelsey." I hold the phone a little too long
before taking it from her.

"You doing okay?" She walks over and sits next to me

on the curb. "I saw, you know, you posting about Frankie and vice versa . . ."

"Ah." I nod. "Yeah, I'll be okay."

"I hope so." She smiles, and there's a pause there before she looks away toward the growing rally. Our classmates, some teachers it seems, a few adults.

"You know, I have never had good timing," she says, laughing a little. "Not ever. It's just not my thing. Even with you, back at summer camp."

I immediately feel my entire body blush. "Kels—"

"It's fine." She laughs more. "But I think about those truth-or-dare games a lot, how I never quite got dared to do the one thing I wanted to."

Kiss me.

She's going to say something about kissing me.

She looks at me, smirks again, and doesn't say it.

But she doesn't have to.

"I know now isn't the time for . . . well, anything." She exhales. "But maybe down the line, eventually, it will be? It could be? You live your truth out loud, even though the people around you, your family, don't want you to."

She looks right at me.

"You want to talk about truth or dare? *That's* fucking daring. And I'd love to hold your hand sometime."

Chapter Twenty-Seven

Bella

I'm late.

My stomach is churning. The rally technically started ten minutes ago, and Frankie and all the other girls have been absolutely blowing up my phone, but . . . the idea that I might show up to this thing, early or on time, with no one else there was too much to bear. What if no one comes? What if no one actually cares, despite how much Frankie and Jo keep insisting they do?

I mean, it's hard to believe anyone *would* care, when Frankie straight up ran away from town, when all this was still so up in the air. And if people do come, are they here for me, or are they here because of Nick?

I know he finally said something. Spoke up. I saw online that he went to the police, finally gave a proper statement. It was hard not to hear about it; everyone I know sent me the link to the article, links to his social media updates. And screenshots of the backlash, people furious that he took his time, that he stood by, that he could have done something.

A statement and a broad apology don't change the fact that he didn't say anything earlier. That he still hasn't really said anything to me, not directly. This doesn't wash his hands clean or buy my forgiveness.

I round a corner, the last line of houses fading into storefronts and boutiques, and . . .

There they are.

All at once, there they are.

There's got to be at least fifty people out here, and I squint to see who I can make out in the crowd as I get closer to the town square, a large statue of Andrew's great-grandfather smack in the middle of it all. I don't even know what the guy did, but I want to topple the thing that bears his name so badly. He's on a horse with a shovel in his hand, and I wonder how he'd feel knowing his great-grandson dug his own grave.

Someone I don't know makes eye contact with me as I get closer and rushes into the group of people, returning quickly, Frankie in tow. Her eyes are just all lit up at the sight of me, a bunch of poster boards duct taped to what look like broomsticks, under her arm.

"You're here," Frankie says breathlessly. She stops, her hands in front of her awkwardly. "Can I give you a hug?"

"Yeah?" I shrug, and Frankie ropes her arms around me.

"I'm sorry," she says, pulling back, and she's biting at her lip. "I know—I know you needed me and we had this to plan, and I just . . . I ran."

"It's fine."

"It's not, though." She riffles through the signs and

then holds them all out to me. "Your choice. I should have squashed my own selfish needs and focused on the bigger picture. Just like . . . well, you know—"

"Nick." I pluck out a sign: black poster board with white lettering that has icy blue shading on it, reading MY BODY IS FROZEN, THANKS TO YOU. "Wow."

"I think Jo drew that one," Frankie says, her eyes searching the letters.

"Are you two . . . okay?" I ask, slinging the protest sign over my shoulder like a rifle.

"No." She sighs. "No, we're not. But that's not what's important right now."

"Well, if you want to talk about it after all this." I reach out and grab her shoulder. "It's important to me."

She smiles like her face might break, and I pull her in for a hug.

"This next part," Frankie says into my shoulder, muffled a little before stepping away. "This next part is going to be really hard, Bella. You know that, right?"

I nod.

"Do you want me up there with you?" Frankie asks. "Me, Jo, you've got a bunch of people here who are here for you, supporting you. Just let me know what you need."

"Where is Jo?" I ask, looking around her. "I know you two aren't great, but she's here?"

"She's on stage detail." She nods toward the statue.

"All right, well, if you want to stay up there with me, I'd . . . I'd like that."

A few people clear out of the way in the milling about crew of supporters. There's a small stage and podium up on the edge of the square. Well, calling it a podium is a bit generous. It looks like a large amplifier case, standing up on its side, and I spot the owner of the local guitar shop, Mr. Tiberia, leaning outside of his store. There's a microphone on top of the case strung to a small speaker—I wonder if it's a guitar amp.

Sure enough, Jo is up there, fussing with the amp. I can't even imagine what her family thinks about her being here, and then she's also got to deal with Frankie being around. I'm glad she's here.

"It's time," Frankie says, a hand on my shoulder. "But only if you're ready."

"I am."

I'm not.

"I really am."

I walk with Frankie toward the little stage, a few people around us saying little encouraging things as we go. As a few more people move out of the way, I see Jo on the stage, sitting on the edge of it, a sign in one hand, her phone in the other. She looks tired. I get myself situated in front of the little makeshift podium and clear my throat. I tap the microphone, the muffled thumps sounding from the amp.

"I almost didn't do this, you know," I start. I look back to Frankie and over to Jo, the two of them looking at me from their separate places near the stage. "But that's this town, isn't it? We all carry our secrets, our hurt. And so many of us are taught, from a young age, to just bury all that down. That it's better to just move on from whatever it is. A disappointed parent. Heartbreak. Sickness. Just . . . shake it off.

"But that doesn't work. And the longer you swallow your feelings, the harder it is to do. It becomes a . . . jagged little pill stuck in your throat. And I'm just not willing to sit here and choke on what I'm feeling anymore. Because I'm *angry*. And I shouldn't have to just take it."

Someone cheers in the audience, and something just catches in my chest.

And I want to ride that energy.

So I push.

"This rally isn't just about me," I say a bit louder now. "You should all know that. It's about all of you. Those of you who are also carrying around this kind of hurt, an assault. We won't be ignored. Negated. Discounted. It's our turn to be heard. We'll take our signs and chants to the streets of Greenport, from here to the most tucked away suburb to downtown and city hall, till our signs fall apart and our feet ache.

"Andrew Montefiore didn't care that I couldn't say no. He left me there on that bed when he was finished with me, and he took a photo." I grit my teeth. "A photo. Well, smile, Andrew. You're about to have company. We walk."

I jump off the stage to the sound of applause from the growing crowd, wiping at the tears on my face. Frankie quickly follows and wraps her arms around me, and so does Jo, and I exhale in the warmth of this crew of girls.

Abruptly, Jo lets go, her movements quick and urgent, and she steps around me and Frankie.

"What are you doing here?" she snaps.

I glance around her, and there's Nick, standing right there, seemingly all ready to go. He can't quite look at me; his eyes keep shifting around everywhere, like he's embarrassed. It's the same look he used to have when we'd stand in the hallways, him nursing his crush on me, only this time . . . it's not because of something he hasn't done but because of something he has. Instead of feeling awkward about not whispering how he feels, he went ahead and yelled it, without saying a damn thing.

That he didn't actually care about me—or any of the other girls standing here with me—through his inaction.

"Bella, I—"

"No one wants you here," Jo says, taking a step toward him. He tries to walk around her, but she nudges him off. "Go home."

"Jo, come on, I just want . . . Frankie," Nick tries.

I look at Frankie, who shakes her head. "Not my call, Nick."

I step away from Frankie, and Jo turns to me, her eyes hard.

"It's okay, Jo," I say, walking around her.

"Bella—" Nick tries to start again.

"Why didn't you stop him?" I ask. A flash of heat flushes my cheeks, a mix of rage and a sob that wants to battle its way out of my chest. But I won't let it. Not because I want to hold back, but because he doesn't deserve these tears.

"I don't know," Nick says, twisting his foot into the asphalt. "But everyone knows now. Right? Everyone knows the truth."

"Yeah, because *you* said it, Nick," I say, taking a step toward him. "It wasn't enough for me to say it, for me to head to the police station and speak my truth. It took you. You get to be the hero now. Like always. Because of who you are, because of what you look like. They believe you."

"I'm sorry!" he exclaims, his face twisting as he starts crying. "If I could change anything, anything, I would go back and—"

"You know what? So would I," I say. "I don't get to do that, though. I don't get to hit reset. You do, and that's messed up."

I swing the sign over my shoulder again.

"Now pick up a fucking sign."

Chapter Twenty-Eight

Frankie

I'm standing on the landing of our staircase and can hear Mom fussing about in the kitchen, muttering to herself.

Sigh.

It begins.

"You gonna move, or are we just going to let Mom's breakfast get cold?" Nick leans over my shoulder and smells the air. "Did she make bacon?"

"You'll never know." I jab him in the chest with an elbow, and he crumples to the floor as I hurry down the stairs. I take the jump he usually does, landing in the living room near the front door with a slam, and hurry around toward the kitchen.

"Noooo . . ." I hear him groan out feebly upstairs.

The bacon will be mine.

I reach the kitchen, and Mom is sitting there in front of her laptop next to Dad, sipping on his coffee. A tablet and a newspaper are sprawled out over the table, and a spread of spectacularly unhealthy bacon and piles of pork roll and scrambled eggs is in the middle.

"Hey, sweetheart," Mom says. "Help yourself. Coffee is on the counter."

I hear the thump of Nick landing in the living room, and he walks into the kitchen, scowling at me playfully. I reach between Mom and Dad and grab a handful of bacon, taking a bite out of several strips at once. He laughs and shakes his head.

"All right," Mom says, rubbing her hands together. "Ready?"

Dad turns around and looks at me and then my brother, his eyes communing everything he needs: "Humor. Her. For. The. Love. Of. God."

Got it, Dad.

"Welcome to the annual Healy holiday letter," Mom starts, leaning against Dad's shoulder as she reads. "I've decided to go digital this year, to save the trees, Christmas or otherwise. Where to begin . . . I'm in awe of my daughter, Frankie. It took me forty years to be as brave as she is at just seventeen. She is an incredible young woman who has inspired me to take action and educate myself in ways that sometimes feel uncomfortable, because they should."

I stop midchew and look up at Nick. He looks just as surprised.

"On top of handling high school and her new part-time job at the women's shelter in Lansburg, the town over, she has spent the last year traveling and protesting in support of Black lives, and doing everything she can to bring justice to her friend Bella Fox, who is a rape survivor, much . . ." Dad hugs Mom from the side, his eyes looking at the screen. "Much like myself."

I glance back at Nick, who stands awkwardly at the kitchen counter. He's looking down at his feet. It's been a hard year for him. His eyes flit up to me and over to Mom and Dad. I motion for him to walk over, and he pulls up a chair across from our parents. Mom looks up at him and reaches out, grabbing his hand.

It's weird. This space. Lingering between anger and for-giveness, disappointment and pride. When do you move closer to one and further from the other? When does this limbo go away? And not just with Nick and Bella, but with me and Jo. Or even Phoenix. We text, make small talk, but that fire that fueled our connection is gone. He's around, though, and that'll have to be enough for now.

Everyone's hurt each other. We're covered in Band-Aids, but healing is going to take a long time.

And I think that's okay.

"As you may have heard, Bella's case is going to trial. The defendant still got into a good college, even under the circumstances. He's sticking to his story, but Bella gets to tell hers, which feels like a win in itself, because most of us never do."

And Mom starts crying. She leans into Dad, and Nick shifts about awkwardly in his seat. Dad glances up at this and flashes his wide eyes at us. But I have no idea what to say here.

Except maybe I kind of do?

It's the same thing I've been talking to Mom about over the course of the year.

"You know, Mom, I didn't really know what you were going through," I say, walking over next to her. "I don't know, sometimes I think I wasn't looking at you as a person. If that makes sense."

"You're my kid." She sniffles. "Most people don't realize their parents are people, or even know their parents, until . . . well, it's too late. Or almost too late. When we adopted you, I just wanted you to feel like you fit in here."

"Or *you* wanted me to fit in here." I wince, trying to be gentle but speaking my truth. "The thing is, I didn't want that."

"I got it wrong."

"Yeah, you did. And it hurt me. But . . . I love you."

"I know. I love you too," she says, swiping at a tear. "I'm going to keep listening, I'm going to try." She glances up at Nick, warmth on her face, and looks back at her laptop and her letter. "Nick is making big decisions for himself now, on his own. He took a year off from college and is appearing as a witness in Bella's case. He can't change what happened, but he's looking inside himself to understand why he didn't do something when he had that chance."

Nick squirms a little in his chair, and Dad reaches out and grabs his hand.

"It's been a big year for my family to figure out who we all are, taking it day by day." She glances at Dad, who squints at the laptop screen and rolls his eyes.

"Come on, MJ," he grumbles.

"I can talk about you all I want in here." She smirks, looking back at the letter. "Steve has started taking guitar lessons, trying to find something else, in addition to his family, outside of work. It's kind of hot—"

I wince and look at Nick, who is also making a face.

"—even though he can only play this one Alanis Morissette riff. We're also in marriage counseling, which I highly recommend, and individual therapy, because we're both messed up and perfectly imperfect people just like all of you. We don't have any secrets anymore."

She takes a deep breath.

"Okay, I think that's enough." She sniffs and moves to shut the laptop. Dad reaches out and stops her.

"It's okay," he says. "If you need this, if you need to get it all out, we're here for it."

Mom looks at me and Nick and then at Dad, her eyes wide, her mouth a thin little line, and turns back to the screen.

"As you all know, I overdosed on fentanyl and oxycodone. I'm sure it was a hot topic at the coffee shop and various PTA meetings, but I don't care. Don't worry, it was exactly as humiliating and messy as you all imagined and probably gossiped about it to be. After they pulled all the tubes out of my body, I went to the Deptford Recovery Center for ninety days. That was the easy part. A few months after I came home, I relapsed—most of us do—and now I'm in an outpatient program. The hard part will be living with this recovery for the rest of my life.

"I didn't expect to make friends there, because I'm that

stuck-up bitch from a Connecticut suburb, but I met some of the kindest people I've ever met. I've lived among all of you in this town and afar for so long that I forgot what empathy felt like."

There's a long pause and Mom glances at all of us.

"Well?" she asks.

"It's great, sweetheart," Dad says. "But you're not actually going to send it like that, are you?"

"Oh, no, you're right." Mom laughs. "It's missing something."

She types something on the screen while reading.

"Love, MJ."

"That's not what I meant." Dad laughs and rubs his hand over his face. Nick snorts out a little chuckle too. "It's just, you're not there anymore, you know? Rock bottom and all. I think you know that, and maybe you think you're still there, but you're not."

"Where am I then?"

"Rock . . . middle?" Nick ventures.

"I'll take that." She smiles.

"Look, I think next year's letter is going to be different," Mom says, looking at the screen. "Maybe not amazing. Maybe not some spectacular humblebrag. But it'll be a little bit better. Every year, every day, is going to get a little bit better. I think this is my last letter, though."

"You're not going to do them anymore?" I ask.

"No," she says. "Because Christmas letters that list all your accomplishments and brag about your family are for assholes."

"Mom!" Nick laughs.

"I dare you to send it," I say, grinning at Mom.

She holds my gaze.

I hold hers.

And with a smirk, she jabs a key.

"Merry fucking Christmas," Mom says, throwing her hands in the air.

"Who did that go to?" Dad asks, laughing.

There's a little pause, and Mom's eyes flit up to mine.

"Everyone."

Lyrics Credits

Dear Reader,

While adapting this musical into a novel, I listened to the cast recording. It made me feel like the characters were right there with me. And now you can hear them while you're reading by going to this link: jaggedlittlepill.lnk.to/OriginalCastRecording!QR. Or point your phone's camera at the QR code below.

Happy reading and listening,
Eric Smith

Acknowledgments

When I was in sixth grade, members of my school chorus were selected to perform in the original Broadway production of *A Christmas Carol* as adorable little angels. We spent evenings at our school in Elizabeth, New Jersey, and, later, in New York City rehearsing for a run that lasted the entire fall and winter.

To say it was a magical time is a wild understatement.

As I grew up, I sometimes thought about maybe one day finding my way back to Broadway. The lights. The music. The permission to daydream. But never in a million years did I see myself doing it through a novel.

Yet here we are. And there are a lot of people to thank for it.

To Alanis Morissette, Diablo Cody, Glen Ballard, Arvind Ethan David, and Vivek J. Tiwary for this wild opportunity. To Maggie Lehrman, who knew how important this story would be to me. To my literary agent, Jennifer Azantian, a guiding light and friend.

To the team at Abrams and Amulet: Gaby Paez, Jenny Choy, Patricia McNamara O'Neill, Kim Lauber, Hallie Paterson, Amy Vreeland, Heather Allen, Andrew Smith, Elisa Gonzalez, Emily Daluga, and Noa Denmon for the gorgeous work on the cover.

To my writer friends Farah Naz Rishi, Lauren Gibaldi,

Tom Torre, Chris Urie, Rebecca Podos, Preeti Chhibber, Swapna Krishna, Laura Taylor Namey, Emily X. R. Pan, Saundra Mitchell, Mike Chen, Mary Kenney, Neil Bardhan, Anna Birch, Rosiee Thor, Olivia A. Cole, Fran Wilde, and Christopher and Shannon Wink for keeping me grounded.

Miguel Bolivar and Darlene Meier, I'd fall apart without you both.

To my colleagues and friends at P.S. Literary. What a team. Thank you for fostering a warm and welcome environment where I can find the time to create.

To my darling wife, Nena Boling-Smith, who had to hear the Broadway cast recording again and again for several months in a row. I love you. To my son, Langston: you are the biggest star in the musical of my life. To my entire family, my parents and my siblings.

And, finally, to Barbara Peraino, Carmen Rooney, and the late Charlotte Cade, my teachers in sixth grade. The ones who got me onstage as a kid and taught me to keep dreaming big about a life in the arts. Mrs. Rooney, I still remember you reading children's books by Barbara Park and Judy Blume to a greenroom full of nervous, terrified kids in order to calm us down before we hit the stage.

I heard every single word.

Thank you, everyone, who daydreamed with me.

About the Creators

ERIC SMITH is a YA author and literary agent with P.S. Literary. His books include *You Can Go Your Own Way*, *Battle of the Bands* (edited with Lauren Gibaldi), *Don't Read the Comments* (a YALSA Best Fiction for Young Adults selection), *The Girl and the Grove*, and *The Geek's Guide to Dating*. Originally from Elizabeth, New Jersey, he now lives in Philadelphia with his family.

Since 1995, **ALANIS MORISSETTE** has been one of the most influential singer-songwriter-musicians in contemporary music. Her deeply expressive music and performances have earned vast critical praise and seven Grammy Awards. Morissette's 1995 debut, *Jagged Little Pill*, has been followed by nine more eclectic and acclaimed albums. Outside of entertainment, she is an avid supporter of female empowerment as well as spiritual, psychological, and physical wellness. On December 5, 2019, *Jagged Little Pill* the musical made its Broadway debut at the Broadhurst Theatre in New York City and subsequently won two Tony Awards. In July 2020, Alanis released her ninth studio album, *Such Pretty Forks in the Road*, to rave reviews. In August 2021, Alanis kicked off her world tour celebrating twenty-five years of *Jagged Little Pill*. Alanis also appeared as a judge on Fox's competition show *Alter Ego*.

DIABLO CODY is the Oscar Award–winning writer and producer best known for *Juno*, *Young Adult*, and *Jennifer's Body*.

GLEN BALLARD is a six-time Grammy producer and songwriter. Over the course of his career, he's worked with some of the biggest names in music, including Alanis Morissette, Michael Jackson, Wilson Phillips, Dave Matthews Band, Quincy Jones, Aerosmith, Annie Lennox, Shakira, and many others.